SPELLING DANGER

CORRINE WINTERS

Join my newsletter by clicking here!

ALSO BY CORRINE WINTERS

Kitten Witch Mystery

Dramatic Paws

Momentary Paws

Temporary Paws

Probable Paws

Sudden Paws

Tricky Paws

Lethal Paws

Perilous Paws

Hidden Paws

Dangerous Paws

Wild Paws

Tart Paws

Mysterious Paws

Familiar Curses Mystery

Witch's Treat

Broom Mates

Witch Please

Occulture Shock

Hex and the City

Witching & Moaning

Life's A Witch

Bottom Witch

Boss Witch

Payback's A Witch

ONE

"Hey, you got plans for the day?" Netta asked, as she and bestie Justine collected empty coffee cups from *The Octopus Inn's* long counter.

Despite the fact that the town of *Siren Key* boasted many coffeeshops, many locals preferred to frequent the inn for a cup of joe and the latest gossip.

Justine sighed and swept aside a lock of her long blond hair that had escaped her bun.

"Hang out here and take care of the joint while you're giving diving lessons and playing in the water," Justine said. "I might try working on my novel more when things slow down a bit."

Netta, who owned the inn, was also a well-known scuba diver who had people from all over the world flocking to her for diving lessons.

"How is the ..."

Netta's question was interrupted when Marliss flung open the front door of the inn, bursting in like an angry tornado bent on destroying everything in its path.

"I thought I would find you here," Marliss screamed at

Kevin Credo. "Drinking coffee and gossiping with your friends until the bars open and you can drink *beer* and gossip with your friends. Did you forget that you have a son?"

Marliss thrust her six-month-old baby at Kevin, pushing the infant in his face. Kevin reached for him, but Marliss snatched him back as though Kevin had some kind of nasty disease.

Then, she slammed a small, crumpled piece of paper on the counter in front of him, knocking over what was left in the coffee cup.

"Your check bounced again," she screamed, as everyone stared in stunned silence. "The baby is out of diapers and I'm having a hard time buying formula and paying my bills, while you play around and party all day.

"I don't care if you don't want to be a part of his life. He's better off with you out of it. But you still have to help me pay for his basic needs."

Justine absentmindedly wiped up the spilt coffee while watching the drama unfolding in front of her.

"You need to calm down, Marliss. You're making a scene," Kevin told her, trying to sound unrattled, although everyone could hear the slight quiver in his voice.

"I'll show you calm down." She picked up a cup of hot coffee from the counter and flung it in his face. "I'll make sure you pay your child support one way or the other. This isn't over."

With that she blew out of the inn as furiously as she had come in.

Kevin stood up quickly, cursing under his breath, knocking the stool over. The loud crash shattered the dead silence and startled everyone in the inn.

Neither Netta nor Justine offered to help. The truth

was that they had very little respect for him. His father was a millionaire, but had cut Kevin off a couple of years ago because Kevin refused to do anything legit to earn his own money. That didn't stop Kevin from acting like he was better than everyone else and that *he* had millions.

Everyone figured that he was just waiting for his daddy to die. But Kevin's father was seemingly very healthy, although there had been rumors here and there about a chronic disease that ailed him. However, it seemed that the elder Credo was likely to be around for a while – unless something unexpected happened to him. Even then, it was rumored that his fortune had been willed to one of his favorite charities.

Netta shook her head, smiled at her friend and said, "You are in charge. I have a diving lesson in half an hour."

"Thanks, I think," Justine said sarcastically, looking at the drenched Kevin still standing there muttering to himself.

Netta patted Justine on the shoulder. Netta instantly had an image of Justine's shocked face pop into her mind. Netta was a witch and was able to see images from the recent past in the form of still photographs. The picture of Justine's face was so funny that she wished that she could frame it. However, as soon as it appeared, it was gone.

Sargasso, a long-haired black kitten and Netta's familiar, followed her closely up the stairs. Once they were in her room, he watched Netta sweep her long, chestnut brown hair up in a bun similar to Justine's. Then, he shook his head as though trying to dispel an image.

"I don't think you should go," he said. "Something doesn't feel right."

Netta knelt down and petted Sargasso.

"I'll be fine. I've done this dive a hundred times," she said.

"I don't like it," the kitten protested, but Netta just smiled at him and headed out. Sargasso always worried about her.

Her client, Dana, was right on time. After Netta showed her the basics and they dove into the water, Netta felt completely at peace. She wondered if she was a mermaid or another sea creature in her past life, as she felt more at home in the water than she did on dry land. It seemed as though even the fish recognized her as a kindred spirit and were not afraid of her. Instead, they swam alongside her like old friends.

Dana learned very quickly, and soon the three-hour lesson was over, which meant that Netta had to return to the real world.

"That was amazing," Dana gushed, once they had taken off all of their gear. "It is an entirely new world under the water. So much beauty and ..." Suddenly she stopped short and turned ghostly white. She started to pant heavily and then she screamed.

Netta stared at her in confusion and then followed her gaze. Bobbing in the water, near Netta's mentor's cabana, was a body posed on a paddle board as though it had been swept in by the tide.

Her heart leapt into her throat, and the serenity she had felt moments ago faded into dread.

Kevin Credo lay on the paddle board as though he were enjoying the morning sun. His wide-open eyes stared at nothing.

TWO

Maven, Netta's mentor and friend, ran out to see what all the commotion was about, and gasped loudly. The body was floating right in front of her shop that sold souvenirs to tourists, as well as a few specialty items to those who knew that she was a witch.

Netta fished her cell phone out of her bag and dialed 9-1-1.

She did her best to describe the situation, but it was difficult. Maven was muttering under her breath about what kind of damage this type of situation would do to her business, while Dana intermittently panted loudly and let out little screams.

Plus, Kevin was posed as though he had just come in from a great time on the water, frozen in place. It was all surreal, and she could barely put together a complete thought.

The operator finally let her get off the phone when they heard the scream of the sirens pulling up to the scene. Three police cars and an ambulance screeched into the parking lot and slammed on their brakes. People in uniforms poured out of the vehicles.

Netta watched the EMTs run over to the body.

It's a little late for them.

She studied the police and detectives as they jumped into action. Then, for the third time that day, her heart nearly exploded into a million pieces.

It seems that the *Siren Key* police force had added a new detective to its ranks.

Danny Sussex.

The same Danny Sussex who had been her love so many years ago during high school, and one of her brother's best friends.

They had talked some, and Netta always had fantasies that someday he would see her as more than just a little sister, and that they would get married and have their two-and-a-third children. It was just a young girl's fairy tale.

Unfortunately, this must have been one of Grimm's tales, because it didn't come true for her.

Danny had left town the day after she graduated from high school to go become a big city cop. Subsequently, she had heard that he left the police force when his partner had been killed while they were tracking down a serial killer.

She had also heard that he had got married and had a daughter. She had never dreamed, in a million years, that he would someday find his way back here.

Netta stood, frozen in complete shock. Memories of Danny and lost dreams floated through her mind as though they were being played back on an old-fashioned reel-to-reel projector.

She had no idea how long she stood there, staring off into space, in a complete daze. One of the officers snapped his fingers in front of her face.

"Miss Netta, are you okay?"

Netta was immediately irritated and slapped his fingers out of her face.

"I'm fine," she said, coldly.

Then, she shook her head, trying to chase the fog away.

"I'm sorry, I was lost in thought. I really don't know anything. I was giving a scuba lesson. He wasn't here when we went into the water about eight. Then, he was there, just as you see him, when we came out of the water around eleven. My client, Dana, saw him almost immediately. I called you guys about a minute later."

Netta told him about the confrontation that happened earlier that day at her inn between Kevin and his baby's mama, Marliss. She told him that she had promised that Kevin would pay his child support one way or the other.

This could certainly be one way to get what she wanted from him.

After a couple more questions, the officer realized that Netta really didn't have any more information than she had given him. He thanked her for her time and walked away.

As she surveyed the scene, and watched more people in various uniforms infiltrate her beloved beach, she felt eyes boring a hole right through her.

She looked up and saw Danny's smoky gray eyes watching her. That same dirty blond curl was in the middle of his forehead, and just like old times, she had a sudden urge to brush it off of his face. However, she certainly wouldn't act on it now.

Netta and Danny locked eyes, and a dozen things flew between them, but Netta couldn't interpret any of them. She suddenly felt like she was a young school girl with a crush again.

Then, he gave her a slight smile, nodded at her, and went back to his work.

Netta walked back toward her inn, praying that her poker face had held. Her throat had tightened and she felt as though her heart was being squeezed by a giant, unseen hand. For a moment, her panic attack felt like a heart attack.

She told herself to get over it. He was a young girl's dream and she was a grown woman now. She needed to get over it.

When she walked into the inn, everyone had questions, but she said that she needed to go upstairs, shower, and change.

Netta sat on her bed and tried to collect her thoughts. It had been a crazy day so far, starting off with Marliss' verbal and physical attack on Kevin with Kevin floating dead in her water, which brought Danny Sussex practically to her door. It wasn't even noon.

Sargasso suddenly appeared next to her, and rubbed against her, trying to comfort her.

"I told you that something bad was going to happen," he said, with just a touch of smugness in his voice.

"But nothing happened to me. I assume that it was me you were worried about and not Kevin," Netta answered.

"This morning it was Kevin," Sargasso said. "But the day is young."

THREE

Danny felt himself go stiff with shock. He knew that he would run into Netta sooner or later. After all, this wasn't that big of a town, even when all the tourists flocked to the beautiful white, Florida beaches when the weather turned nasty elsewhere.

However, he never expected to find her at a murder scene. She was every bit as beautiful as she had ever been. To be honest, he had thought about her once in a while, over the last few years. An occasional "what if" crossed his mind. He had known that she had fancied herself in love with him, and that he had felt affection for her.

He shook his head to banish those thoughts.

First of all, he had felt compelled to get out of *Siren Key*. The town was stifling and he had wanted to see the world – or at least a little more of it.

Second, he would never have had his daughter if he hadn't left, who was the light of his life.

Netta turned to look at him. Danny couldn't read the expression on her face, but figured that she felt the same shock as he did. After all, she might have heard that he was coming back, or she might not have. He figured that he would stop by and see her some time. He knew that she owned the inn that loomed in the background, so she wouldn't be hard to find.

Her blue eyes matched the color of the ocean that she loved so much. He was mesmerized by them. Then, at the same time, they shook off the hypnotic state, and Danny told himself, under his breath, that he had a job to do.

Another detective approached Netta, and Danny turned to talk to Dana, who had been the first person to spot the dead man. She held a paper bag over her nose and mouth, trying to calm her breathing and stop hyperventilating.

He sat beside her and told her kindly that he understood that she had experienced a shock but he really needed to talk to her while everything was fresh in her mind.

She nodded.

"I understand. I've watched *Criminal Minds* and *CSI*. I know how it works," Dana said, her voice shaking so much that Danny struggled to understand her.

It's funny how everyone thinks that real police business is exactly the same as what they see on television. If only they knew.

Danny asked her to describe what happened when they came out of the water. He wanted to know what she saw, what she heard, what she smelled, trying to get her to use all of her five senses.

She had started to calm down a bit, and Dana animatedly described how when she first saw the body, she thought that someone had just come in from paddleboarding. Then, she noticed that he wasn't moving at all. She thought that it was just a statue or some kind of advertisement, then it occurred to her that the man was dead.

"I've never seen a dead person before. Well, I've seen them on television, but not in real life. I didn't get too close to him, because I know that I could mess up evidence, but I don't know how they managed to pose him and get him to stay in that position. Do you know?" Dana asked. She was talking so fast that it was very hard to follow her.

"We're investigating that, but I'm afraid that even if that information was available, I wouldn't be able to share it with you, because this is an ongoing case. I'm sure that once we figure out if this is a murder or something else, and the case is solved, all of the information will come out in the newspapers," Danny told her.

"Of course, I understand," Dana told him. "You're almost as hot as Agent Derrick Morgan," she said, referring to a character on *Criminal Minds.* "Are you busy later?"

Dana had clearly completely overcome her shock of finding the body, since she was now openly flirting with Danny.

"Thanks for the compliment, ma'am. I'm afraid that it is against department policy to have any kind of relationship, except for a professional relationship, with witnesses," Danny said.

He pulled a card out of his pocket.

"Here is my information if you think of anything else."

"Thank you, Detective. Can I go now?" Dana asked, her attitude back to professional, as she apparently didn't like being rebuffed.

"Of course. Thank you for your help," Danny told her.

He shook his head as he watched her head to the inn where she had booked a room. He wondered if she was going to be sticking around for a while, or if the murder had scared her away.

Danny noticed that Netta had left. He would compare

Dana's story with Netta's, although he was positive that they would match. However, he always carefully followed procedure.

Staring at the inn for a moment, he figured that he would stop in after he got his paperwork done to get a cup of coffee and visit with an old friend. He told himself that she was just the little sister of his childhood best friend, and that was all there was to it.

He wondered if that were true.

His attention was brought back to the task at hand as the medical examiner arrived. The ME looked at the body with some surprise. He didn't see a lot of murders in *Siren Key* and the situation surrounding this particular death was very interesting.

Danny approached the man.

"What's going on, Drake?"

"Not much. I heard you were back in town," the ME said.

"It was time," Danny said simply, not offering more of an explanation. "What do you think happened to our friend here?"

"I'll let *you* know as soon as *I* know whether we have a dangerous killer in town," Drake said with a grim smile.

FOUR

Justine reminded Netta that she had some very important guests coming to the inn sooner rather than later. They were a couple of directors thinking about doing a documentary on the best diving spots and instructors in the nation. Netta had caught their attention.

They wanted to check her out for themselves to see if she would be a good feature for their show. They were set to arrive the following morning.

Netta felt ecstatic about the prospect. The directors were well-regarded, and had been in charge of some very lucrative documentaries. This type of publicity could really increase her business. Who knows, she might even be able to expand and hire a couple of local people who were almost as good as she was?

She also had dreams of getting a larger boat so she could take more experienced divers further out to practice deep sea diving.

"I'm going over to *Victor's Italian Delights* to pick up desserts for them," she told Justine. "I'm sorry that you've been here practically all day by yourself, but do you mind holding down the fort just a little bit longer?"

"Of course not," Justine replied. "At least I won't mind if you bring me back some of his lasagna."

"I'll see what I can do," Netta replied. "But isn't that extortion?"

Justine shrugged her shoulders.

"That is the price you gotta pay," in her best Italian gangster voice.

The hostess and Netta had gone to school together. Ginger was a very sweet woman who had a smile for everyone.

"It's great to see you, Netta. More delicious treats for a VIP guest?" Ginger asked.

"You guessed it," Netta said. "Plus, Justine has demanded lasagna as payment for watching the inn this afternoon while I run errands."

Ginger nodded.

"She has excellent taste. The lasagna is especially good today, and I think that Frank has just taken some out of the oven."

While Ginger asked one of the waiters to grab two to-go boxes of lasagna, Netta decided on a couple of delicacies that were decorated with edible gold flakes, a classy touch which was Victor's specialty.

Once she'd placed her order, she stared off into space, thinking about Danny. It had been a shock to see him, even though she'd heard he had come back.

She hadn't expected him to join the police force, although it made sense. He had been a cop in the big city, so it stood to reason he would stay in the same field.

Suddenly, a loud familiar voice broke into her thoughts. Victor was berating Knoll.

"If you want to keep working for me, you had better start making your deliveries on time. I don't care if you are thirty seconds late, that is still late, and it won't be tolerated. If you are late one more time, I'll have your head on a platter."

"Yes, sir. It'll never happen again," Knoll said, so low that Netta barely heard his voice.

Then, Victor turned around and noticed that Netta was standing there. He smiled and held out his hand for her to shake. Netta reluctantly took it, as she had always found Victor to be a little creepy.

"It's good to see you again," Victor said. "You know it's so hard to find good help these days. This is the third time this month that Knoll didn't deliver one of the wedding cakes on time and I had to refund the money. The only reason he still has a job here is because I feel sorry for him. His life hasn't been the easiest."

Netta smiled and nodded.

"That's very kind of you," she said. She didn't really believe in Victor's altruistic motives. There was something in it for him, but it wasn't her business. She was just here for treats and lasagna.

Frank returned with her boxes and Netta paid and headed out the door. She groaned inwardly when she saw that Scylla, a reporter for the local television station, was heading in at the same time.

"Oh hi, Netta," Scylla said in a high-pitched, nasally voice with her trademark valley girl intonation. She twirled her platinum blond hair around her finger and then flung it over her shoulder in an exaggerated model move. "I've been looking all over the place for you. I was so worried about you. I know you must have had a real bad shock when you found that body this morning."

Netta briefly closed her eyes, hoping when she opened them again that Scylla would be gone. Unfortunately, she didn't possess that kind of magic, and wouldn't be able to use it on Scylla even if she did.

"Thank you for your concern, Scylla. I'm fine, but I do have to get back to the inn," Netta said.

"You know that I'm here for you," Scylla said. "We can talk anytime you need."

"Thank you. I'm fine, and I've been instructed not to talk about what happened to anyone anyway," Netta answered.

"Do you have any kind of information you can give me? You know, since we are old friends," Scylla said. "I would love to get a scoop, and I could always attribute it to an anonymous source."

"I really can't," Netta said. All I can say is 'no comment.' Please excuse me. I have a lot of work that I need to get done. I've got some important guests coming.

"By the way, these guests are film directors, and have had a lot of their documentaries shown on *The Discovery Channel*. That would be a great story for you if you are interested."

Then, without waiting for an answer, Netta pushed past Scylla, heading for her car. Netta was pretty sure that Scylla called her a bad word as she left.

Although it wasn't every day that *Siren Key* had a murder, Netta was actually more in shock that she had seen Danny, than a dead body posed on a surfboard.

But Danny Sussex wasn't a subject that she wanted to discuss with Scylla, either.

FIVE

Netta was exhausted by the time that she returned to the inn. It had been a long, dramatic day. She really wanted to put the cakes up in the kitchen, deliver the lasagna, and take a nap. However, as it was only about two in the afternoon, the chances of that happening were just about nil.

She wasn't surprised to see Emily, their resident ghost, hanging out with Justine. Justine's novel was based on Emily's life. She had died of a broken heart a couple of centuries ago when her fiancé and the love of her life had died at sea. She had only been eighteen.

However depressed she had been when she had died, she was very sweet and cheerful now as she went about her ghostly life, like most of the local residents of *Siren Key,* alive or not. Emily loved Justine, Sargasso, and Caspia—the familiar-in-training white kitten.

Emily was telling Justine about the local gossip. Everyone was talking about Kevin and how he had been boasting that he was about to come into a lot of money.

"People are saying that he thought his father had

cancer, and because he was about to die, Kevin thought that his father had changed his will back to him. We *all* know that every bit of the money is going to the local animal shelter." Emily rolled her eyes, emphasizing the point that Kevin wasn't the sharpest tack in the corkboard.

"Kevin's daddy looks very healthy," Justine said.

"I *know,*" Emily said, talking like a modern-day teenager. "Now that Kevin's dead, everybody is saying that he was involved in the drug trade. He probably was taking his own products, which would explain how a thirty-five-year old man would drop dead while paddle boarding. Or maybe he just owed the drug dealers money."

"Basically, it is a whole lot of gossip. In reality, no one really knows anything," Netta said.

"I hope it's not drugs," said Justine. "I know that there is no place in the world that doesn't have some drugs. But if the big drug people come here, then our sweet little town will be destroyed."

"Unless we get someone like El Chapo. He supposedly helped out the poor, built schools, hospitals, and lots of other great things. That's why he's a hero to a lot of the Mexican people," Emily said.

"He also murdered a lot of folks, or had them murdered. He killed even more people through the drug trade or because of the drugs themselves. Doing a little bit of good doesn't compensate for doing great evil," Netta said.

Emily nodded.

"That is true," she said. "I guess I never thought of it like that. I figured if people got involved in the drug trade and were killed, then they got what they deserved."

"There are many people who would agree with you," Netta said. "And perhaps that is one form of justice. But two wrongs do not make a right."

Again, Emily nodded.

"What about the argument that if it wasn't El Chapo, it would have been someone else who was running the drugs? Someone who was even more evil and who wouldn't have helped the people at all?"

"That is also a point that people make. But even if we can argue that there are different degrees of evilness, which I'm not sure I agree with, that doesn't excuse the devastation he caused millions of people, whether they were killed by violence or by drugs."

Justine broke in.

"These are really great arguments and the debate is interesting, but if drugs didn't kill Kevin, what did?"

"Marliss was plenty angry this morning," Emily said. "I watched their whole argument from the corner, making sure that no one could see me. You never know who can see us and who can't."

"She was angry, but angry enough to kill someone? Even Kevin? There were no marks on him. No knife wounds, no gunshots, so I'm not sure how she would have done it," Justine said.

Netta gave Justine a strange look.

"How do you know all that about the condition of his body?"

Justine looked guiltily over at Emily, who looked at the ceiling.

"Oh, look at the time," she said, and started to fade away.

"Oh, no, you don't," Netta said. "You come back here, right now."

Emily sighed.

"As soon as I heard the commotion, I went over to the body. There wasn't any blood on him anywhere. I heard the

ME, Drake, talking about it. He was confused. Then, I *might* have come over to talk to Justine about what I saw and heard."

"How many other people did you tell?" Netta asked.

"No one. I promise, cross my heart, and hope to die," Emily said.

Netta gave her a stern look.

"You've already died."

"I'm speaking figuratively. I know that the police always hold back information from the public. I wouldn't tell anyone," Emily said earnestly.

About that time, Sargasso apparated into the inn, next to Emily. The back half of a white kitten also appeared. Then, that half disappeared and the other half showed up. That was gone and then a tail and a set of ears appeared.

Sargasso was trying to teach Caspia how to apparate, and the apprentice was slowly getting the hang of it. It usually took her several tries before she appeared in full.

Finally a beautiful, pure white kitten appeared.

"Whew," she gasped. "I didn't think that I was ever going to be whole again!"

Justine picked her up and stroked her.

"Everything takes practice. I've been practicing my magic my whole life and I still haven't figured out how to control it. You're still a baby and you're doing a whole lot better than I am."

Netta was glad that all the talk about murder had been put aside for now. She was ready to focus on something else. Anything else.

Even though she knew it would come back to haunt her.

Just like our resident ghost, she thought. *But far less charming...*

SIX

anny felt frustrated and wanted to literally tear
out his hair.

They wouldn't talk to him.

They didn't know anything about anything, didn't know anyone, and couldn't help in any way. They were very polite as they closed their doors in his face.

People knew who he was. He had grown up in the town. However, they considered him to be something of an outsider, and perhaps even a traitor. It seemed that the general consensus was that when you left, you were supposed to stay gone.

He probably would have 'stayed gone' if it hadn't been for two factors.

The first was that Naomi, his wife, died.

They had fallen completely in love, despite the fact that he was mortal and she a witch. Danny had been over the moon when Naomi had given birth to Ayla.

Then, when Ayla was only three years old, Naomi had been murdered. The cause of death was something of a mystery, as there seemed to be a laser burn through her heart. But the ME couldn't determine what kind of weapon would make that mark. Of course, no one saw anything or anyone.

Luckily, Ayla was at a friend's house, so she wasn't hurt in any way.

The second factor was that his police partner had been killed and Danny had been shot. They were after a serial killer who thought they were getting too close.

Danny and Seth had stepped out of their car when they heard two cracks in the air. The first crack sent Seth to the ground. He died immediately from an armor-piercing round. Then, a second crack heralded a round that went through Danny's shoulder.

Danny had felt lost. Seth had been his best friend in Miami. As a matter of fact, when the shooting occurred, Ayla had been at Seth's house, playing with his twins of the same age under the watchful eye of his wife.

Soon after this second tragedy, once he'd talked over the situation with his parents, Danny decided that it was time to come home.

He arrived back in *Siren Key* with a bullet hole in his shoulder and a six-year-old daughter with the biggest blue eyes anyone had ever seen.

Ayla was the light of his life. After Naomi died, his daughter had become his entire world. She was a strange little thing, though, with an incredible talent she'd clearly inherited from her magicker mom.

She loved plants and had a magical green thumb. Literally. She would talk to plants, coo at them and sing to them, and even the sickliest would suddenly come alive and thrive.

This morning, Danny had left Ayla with his parents,

who were excited to spend a lot of time with their beloved granddaughter. He had nothing to worry about there, except maybe they would spoil her too much.

His mother had some plants that weren't doing as well as she had hoped. He knew that Ayla was fascinated by them, so shortly, they would grow by leaps and bounds.

Huge plants made Danny think about the musical *Little Shop of Horrors,* and he decided that the one plant that he would never get Ayla was a Venus Flytrap. She would have that thing gobbling up all the townsfolk in no time.

Danny's cell phone rang, making him spill soda on his trousers. It was the ME. Danny and Drake had been good friends in high school and played four years of football together, along with Netta's brother, James.

"Hey, Drake. How are things?" Danny asked.

"Good, you?" Drake asked.

"Frustrated. No one will give me the time of day. I should have figured that I would get that kind of a reception when I returned," he groaned.

"Give them time. They'll get over themselves. Meanwhile, I have some information that might help you," Drake said.

"Please. I could use it right about now," Danny said.

"I examined Kevin's lungs and ran some other tests when I couldn't find an immediate cause of death. He didn't test positive for any of the normal poisons that kill people. So, I sat down with my handy dandy medical book to try to figure out what was going on," Drake said, pausing for effect.

"What did you find out?" Danny tried very hard not to sound impatient.

"Before I give you the *big* news, I will tell you that there was a metallic substance around his neck, as though someone tried to strangle him with something and metal flakes rubbed off. I will have to run more tests to figure out what it is," Drake said.

"And now for the big news. It turns out that our boy was murdered with ricin gas."

Danny was silent for a moment, in complete shock. That wasn't what he had expected to hear.

"Isn't that made out of castor beans? And popular with terrorists?" Danny asked.

"It is," Drake said.

"So, Kevin was killed by terrorists?"

"Not necessarily. Ricin gas isn't hard to make. The directions are on the internet if you know where to look, and there are definitely some bad people out there who know *exactly* where to look," Drake said.

"That is one of the downfalls of the information highway. You can learn how to do anything from crocheting to making a bomb."

"So anyone who can read and knows how to get around on the internet could have killed him?" Danny groaned.

"Pretty much, yes."

"Were there any drugs in his system?" Dany inquired.

"Nope. We ran the tests looking for all of the usual suspects. He hadn't done any kind of illegal drugs for at least the last thirty days. We could test his hair, but I suspect we would find out that he wasn't a drug user," Drake said.

"If you wouldn't mind, can you test his hair just so we can dot our i's and cross our t's? Were you able to determine the time of death?" Danny asked.

"Yes, roughly around eight in the morning. He hadn't digested any of the blueberry breakfast muffin that he had eaten at *The Octopus Inn*," Drake reported.

"Where in the world would he have been exposed to ricin gas so soon after leaving the inn?" Danny asked himself, aloud.

"I don't know but I urge you to find out soon. Before more bodies show up."

SEVEN

Netta was standing at *The Octopus Inn's* counter, pouring a coffee refill for Old Pete, a lonely regular who stopped by most afternoons just for the company, when Danny walked in. Justine nudged her with her elbow. Netta looked up and drew in a sharp breath. Her hand jerked and she spilled coffee all over the counter.

"That's starting to be a trend," Justine muttered, grabbing a towel to wipe up the mess.

Danny walked over to Netta.

"It's been a long time."

Netta felt as though her throat had closed up and she couldn't get any words out, so she simply nodded.

"Can I get you a cup of coffee or a danish?" Justine jumped in.

"A cup of coffee would be nice. No danish, though. I need to talk to Netta about something," Danny said.

"Y'all go sit down and talk," Justine said, pouring him a cup. "Pete and I will hang out here."

Netta led Danny to a corner booth. Emily and the cats

brazenly followed, wanting to know what was going on. Since the mortal Danny couldn't see Emily and would think that the cats were—well—just cats, they could eavesdrop with impunity.

There was an awkward silence before Danny spoke again.

"I need your help. No one around here will give me the time of day. They look at me suspiciously, as though I could be the killer. If you were to come with me, they might open up a little bit more.

"Everyone knows we used to be close, so it would make sense if you and I hang out together."

"I'm not a detective. It wouldn't make sense for me to... To be with you while you are trying to talk to people... While you're investigating a crime," Netta stammered.

She really didn't want to spend time with Danny. She didn't have time or headspace to think about him or her broken heart.

"Consider yourself a consultant. I can tell people that, if they ask why you are with me, although I doubt that anyone will question it," Danny said.

"I don't have time. I have two businesses to run. Plus, I have some powerful directors coming into town. I need to convince them to include me in their documentary," she protested. "There are plenty of other people who could do a better job of helping you out."

Danny leaned in close.

"Kevin was poisoned with ricin gas."

A confused look crossed Netta's face.

"Isn't that what terrorists use?"

"Yes, and apparently, it is very easy to make with just a few common ingredients. We can't let a crime like this go unsolved for very long. It will scare everyone half to death and ruin the reputation of our little town.

"Your businesses would go under and the directors certainly wouldn't want to film anything here," Danny said, trying hard to make his case. "I don't need all of your time. Just a couple of hours here and there.

"You're the only person that I know here that I can completely trust. I need your help. Please."

Netta considered, biting the inside of her lip.

"Fine," she said finally. "I'll help you, I guess. But only because I care about this town and all of the people in it. We can't have people being killed and we can't have everyone in town losing their businesses."

"Thank you," Danny said. "I really appreciate it. Do you have some time right now? I wanted to go talk to Marliss—"

He stopped in the middle of his thought as Scylla pranced into the room, her platinum blond ponytail bouncing behind her.

"Danny, I was looking everywhere for you," Scylla said, in her valley girl voice. "I just found out some news that would help you close this case in a jiffy."

Then, she looked over at Netta, as if she hadn't noticed her before.

"Oh, hi Netta. I see you two are getting reacquainted."

Netta just rolled her eyes.

"What news do you have for me?" asked Danny.

"Well, it seems that Marliss had taken out a million-dollar life insurance policy on Kevin a couple of months ago. Now that he is dead, she wants to collect. About an hour after Kevin's body was found, she called up the insurance company and told them that she wanted her money," Scylla purred.

"How did you learn this information?" Danny asked.

"Oh, I have a friend who works for the insurance company," Scylla practically purred. "So Marliss came in here the morning Kevin died and threatened him. She told him that she would get the money from him one way or another. Then, he dies. Right after that, she wants to collect on the life insurance policy!

"I just solved your case for you. It's my *welcome home* present to you, all wrapped up in a bow," Scylla cooed.

"Well, thank you for the tip," Danny said. "I will definitely check it out. However, there is still a lot of investigating to do. Unfortunately, things rarely turn out to be as straightforward as you propose.

"Probably better not to get your hopes up for an easy solve."

"Maybe I can get an exclusive with you after everything is wrapped up? After all, I'm not an active part of the investigation, right?" Scylla said.

"I'll give you the same information as any other reporter," Danny said. "I'm just a detective. I can't promise you anything more than that."

"Hmph," Scylla said, and tromped out of the inn as though she were a two-year-old throwing a temper tantrum.

"Looks like you don't need my help after all," Netta said, not sure whether to feel disappointed or relieved.

"Not so fast," Danny murmured. "Scylla actually offered us an interesting lead, and I will definitely check it out.

"I just don't want her, or anybody else, to expect miracles."

EIGHT

Danny hoped that Scylla had offered them a solid lead, although he knew from long, bitter experience that when it came to murder, things were never as simple as they seemed.

Reaching out to Netta was not an easy decision, because he still wasn't sure how he felt about her. He needed time and space to think about it, and then figure out where to go from there. He suspected that she still had some feelings for him, but he would never assume.

He had thought about Netta off and on over the years since Naomi had died, but his main focus had been on his daughter. Ayla seemed well-adjusted and happy, so he figured that he had done a decent job.

Until they became comfortable together, either as a couple or just as friends, it would be a little awkward working with her. However, she was well-known and well-liked in town, and witnesses would be more likely to open up to her.

Danny smiled at Netta and asked if she wanted to go visit Marliss with him. She sighed and agreed.

She looked over at Justine, silently asking that Justine watch over everything. Justine nodded.

A few minutes later, Marliss drew in a deep breath when she saw Danny and Netta at her door. She opened it wider.

"Come in. I've been expecting you."

She looked at Netta a little curiously.

"Netta, I'm sorry for making a scene and a mess at your inn this morning. I was just so frustrated, I wasn't even thinking," Marliss said, sounding truly apologetic.

"You just spilled a little coffee. You didn't throw stools or break anything, so it's all good," Netta smiled at her. "Besides, there are several people who wanted to do the same thing to Kevin, or worse, and they didn't have nearly as good a reason as you did.

"I'm just here as a liaison between you and Detective Sussex."

That seemed to make sense to Marliss. Danny looked around the apartment and noted that it was clean but shabby. He assumed it was the best that she could do on her pay and tips from the café, and what little bit of money Kevin had given her.

"I didn't kill Kevin," Marliss told Danny before he could open the conversation. "Scylla has already been here asking me a bunch of questions. I didn't tell her anything. But I know that means that you're already aware of the life insurance policy, because Scylla spreads news faster than social media."

Danny smiled at her and nodded.

"That's why I am here. I wanted to ask you about the life insurance policy."

Marliss swallowed. Netta noticed that her hands trembled, so much so that Marliss' cell phone slipped from her grasp and clunked to the floor. Netta picked it up and handed it back to the anxious woman, who smiled gratefully.

"I would never have killed Kevin," Marliss said. "I did take the insurance policy out on him, though. I had heard that he was taking drugs and maybe even selling them. People in the drug trade don't last very long.

"If Kevin was killed, I knew I would never get any help supporting the baby, because his father doesn't like me. If I pushed the issue, then Kevin Sr. would go to court to take away Kevin III. And he would win because I can't afford an attorney," Marliss said, wiping a tear from her face.

"I can't lose my baby," she said, the fear and anxiety evident on her face.

"I understand," Danny said. "It's obvious that you love him and that you're a great mother."

"I loved Kevin, too," Marliss said. "He was great at first, and then he became abusive. He hit me when I was pregnant, and I almost lost the baby. That's why we separated. I wasn't going to live like that and I wasn't about to subject my baby to that."

"So you went to the insurance agent today to try to get the money?" Danny asked.

Marliss nodded.

"Yes. I am broke right now and the baby needs some stuff."

Netta opened her purse and pulled out two twenties, which was all she had.

Marliss protested.

"I can't take money from you," she said.

"Call it a loan, if you want," Netta smiled at her. "The baby is adorable, and it takes a village to raise a child. I'm part of your village."

"Thank you," Marliss said, spontaneously hugging Netta.

Danny believed Marliss, but he couldn't just go on his gut feelings. He had to put his trust in evidence, and Marliss was still the number one suspect in the case. She certainly had the motive.

"I'm going to have to ask you to not leave town until we get this case solved," Danny told Marliss.

Marliss laughed without humor.

"Until I get the money from Kevin's life insurance policy, I don't have enough to go *across* town, let alone out of town."

Danny nodded.

"We'll get this solved as soon as we can so that you can collect."

"Thank you. Once that happens, I am taking the baby and going as far away from Kevin Sr. as I possibly can so he won't ever find us," Marliss said. "He is as much of a monster as his son was.

"I didn't kill Kevin, but I'm not in the least bit sorry that he is dead. I'd like to shake the hand of the person who did kill him." Bitterness, fear, and animosity was very evident in Marliss' voice.

"Thank you for your time, ma'am," Danny said, clearly feeling as though there was nothing more to be learned from her.

Once they were in his car and heading back to the inn, Danny asked Netta what she thought about the situation.

"The baby is adorable, and it's obvious that he's well-loved," was all she said.

Great. Not even the person who is supposed to be helping me trusts me.

Not for the first time, Danny worried about his latest life choice.

Had he made a mistake coming back to *Siren Key*?

NINE

Netta had mixed feelings about Marliss. She knew the other woman loved that baby immensely. She didn't think that Marliss was the kind of person who would ordinarily kill someone.

However, if that someone posed a threat to a child, people could do the unthinkable.

Statistically speaking, women killers tended to prefer poisons over other means of homicide, and ricin had proven an especially effective murder weapon. The gas only took a couple of ingredients to make, and depending on the dosage, the effects would be immediate.

Also, ricin wasn't one of the toxins that a medical examiner would automatically test for during an autopsy.

Kind of a genius move on the killer's part.

All of those considerations moved Marliss to the top of the suspect list.

On the other hand, Marliss was too good of a mother to make a deadly poison in her kitchen. It would be a huge risk for her son. But Marliss could have created the poison in a secondary location.

And Marliss was very, very angry with Kevin.

One thing that Netta did know was, contrary to what their prime suspect had said, Marliss was planning on leaving town soon.

When Netta had touched Marliss' phone, her ability to see past events kicked in. She suddenly visualized two boarding passes and a red, white, and blue logo.

Marliss had booked airline tickets for herself and the baby.

But Netta hadn't seen the pair's destination nor the exact departure date. And she didn't dare tell Danny how she'd gathered this critical piece of evidence.

Obviously, Danny had known and accepted that his wife was a witch, and that his daughter possessed certain powers.

But did he know about Netta's magical nature?

She couldn't very well just come out with it. *By the way, I'm a witch, too, but only a couple people know so you can't tell anyone. I see the past in snapshots. And while we're talking about it, I saw that ...*

Netta decided all she could do was to give him a hint. As she exited the car, she blurted it out.

"You should check out the bus stations and airports to see if Marliss was being honest about not leaving town. I have a gut feeling that she isn't going to risk Kevin's father trying to take the baby away from her. Scared people tend to run."

Danny nodded.

"That's a great idea."

Netta watched Danny leave. Then she walked down to the beach where Kevin's body had been found, to see if she could sense anything or pick up any overlooked clues.

She knelt down in the sand and closed her eyes. The

warm sun soothed her and wrapped around her like a blanket. She almost felt as though she could go to sleep right where she was.

Slowly moving her hand over the sand, like a metal detector searching for treasure, a cold chill traveled through her body. Suddenly, an image of a gold bar popped into her head.

But before she could really focus on it, it started to fade away. She could see letters on the gold bar, but they disappeared before she could read them.

Frustrated, she walked back to the inn. Justine sat at the lobby counter, staring off into space, as though in a trance.

Worried, Netta asked her if she was okay, but Justine didn't seem to hear her. She seemed focused on an image no one else could see.

I can relate, Netta thought wryly.

She put her hand on Justine's shoulder and gently shook her. Snapping out of her trance, Justine stared at Netta with wide, frightened eyes.

"Danger is on the way. You are in danger," Justine said, in a low, far-away-sounding voice.

"What do you mean?" Netta frowned.

Justine shook her head, and a tear of frustration formed in her eye.

"I don't know. I *never* know. Do you think that I will ever be able to control my talents?" she asked.

Justine was a latent witch, able to see future events via brief trances. However, she had not yet learned to control when she went into the trances, and sometimes her visions didn't make sense until the event was upon her.

"Honey, I don't know. All I can tell you is to just keep practicing and working with Maven," Netta said.

"Ugh," Justine answered.

Netta just laughed a little. Justine's struggle to figure out how to use her powers was a constant source of irritation to her lovely, talented, friend.

"Speak of the devil," Justine muttered.

"I heard that, you little monster," Maven said, as she entered the inn. "I am a witch, and sometimes I'm grumpy, but I am not the devil."

Justine and Netta laughed. Maven put out a very cranky air, but underneath all of the burrs, she was a loving person who would bend over backwards for anyone.

"Maven, let me get you some cocoa. You look like you've been through the wringer," Netta said.

"Better add whisky to that cocoa," said Maven.

Netta sighed and laughed.

"You know we don't allow alcohol in the inn. So what in the world happened to you?"

Maven's hair looked wild. Her short gray curls seemed to be going in every direction, like little snakes trying to escape her head. Her eyes were wide, and her lips were pressed tightly together.

"That Scylla won't leave me alone. She has been hounding me all morning for a statement. Anything for her magazine.

"She wants to know what I saw, what I heard, and how I felt to have a dead body found so close to my cabana," Maven said.

"What did you tell her?" Justine asked.

"I told her to bug off and leave me alone, I don't have time for her," Maven said. "She followed me around all afternoon, and even harassed a couple of my customers. That was all I could take. I kicked her out and came over here."

"We are always glad to see you," Netta said.

"The next time I see that annoying creature, I'm going to turn her into a frog," Maven declared stoutly.

TEN

Netta and Justine smiled at each other when they heard Maven's declaration. Maven was certainly a very powerful witch and could easily turn Scylla into a frog.

However, every magicker knew that good witches didn't do things like that. They could only use their gifts for positive purposes. Turning someone into an amphibian wasn't a positive use.

The younger witches hadn't even voiced their concerns before Maven went on the defensive.

"Don't you smile like that," Maven snapped, and her hair snakes roiled in agitation. "Turning someone into a frog is the perfect use of my powers. We have a lot of sand fleas that annoy people around here, and an extra mouth to help eliminate those little pests would benefit the community as well as the people who want to use the beach at night.

"It would also be a positive act because then Scylla wouldn't annoy people like us who just want to live our lives in peace without someone constantly asking us for information."

Netta and Justine stayed silent. Despite Maven's lawyerly reasoning, the transformation still wouldn't be allowed by any self-respecting witch, because it wouldn't be a positive change for Scylla. And Maven would see that, in time.

Maven was Netta's mentor, and Justine's and Ayla's trainer. She was of indeterminate age, but seemed as though she had been around forever. She prided herself on being considered a grumpy old magicker, although everyone in town loved her whether they knew she was a witch or not.

Maven settled into a comfortable chair, and her hair slowly returned to normal, or as normal as it ever got, being stuck to the head of a passionate supernatural being. It curled up against her head and went to sleep.

"Scylla is so annoying. I wish she would have stayed where she was instead of coming back here," Maven said. "Do you know why she returned to harass us instead of remaining in Tampa?"

"I don't know, but I have a feeling we're about to find out," Justine said.

"You're awfully impudent for a witch in training." Maven turned her nose in the air and looked away from Justine.

Netta watched and repressed a chuckle. Justine and Maven always gave each other a hard time. It seemed like they didn't get along, but she knew they'd be lost without each other.

Justine was the daughter that Maven never had, and Maven replaced Justine's parents who had died a long time ago in a freak boating accident.

Maven went on.

"I found out that Scylla had been fired from her last job as a reporter because she actually created situations that she would then scoop to increase her ratings. She got the idea from a TV show.

"Apparently, her crazy scheme worked. Scylla's ratings went up and the cops started to look bad," Maven said, then added dramatically, "Scylla thought that she could become number one on the syndicate: the next Barbara Walters."

Maven's gossip proved so juicy that Emily appeared to listen in. As the others talked about Scylla's checkered past and annoying present, Netta wondered how much of the rumor was true. Many rumors had at least a tiny grain of truth in them.

Could Scylla have arranged for Kevin's murder to further her career?

Ambition did seem to blind a lot of people. They saw only the end of the game and didn't care who they had to hurt to get there.

Scylla was a woman, so poison could be the weapon of choice. She was a reporter, so she would know how to find information about creating ricin gas and where to look for the ingredients. She would also know that ricin gas was not the easiest cause of death to investigate.

The fact that she was so willing to feed tidbits of information to Danny only added fuel to the fire. Killers occasionally put themselves into investigations, not only for the thrill, but also to keep tabs on where the cases were going.

Zeus, a pit bull and Maven's familiar, suddenly appeared next to the old witch, bringing Netta out of her reverie.

"Do you have any snacks?" Zeus asked, getting the most important point of business out of the way first.

Netta produced a couple of pieces of bacon left over from breakfast that she had saved just for Zeus. He often popped in looking for treats.

"You have got to quit feeding that dog," Maven said. "He's already as round as a barrel. It's going to start taking him a week to apparate with all of that mass."

Zeus just sniffed loudly and gulped down the treats.

"I actually came here to tell you that the reporter woman is out there looking around your cabana," grunted the dog in his deep, raspy voice. "She's peeking through the windows."

Maven stood up suddenly, sending her chair flying across the floor.

"That's it. One frog coming up."

Justine and Netta convinced Maven to stay put while Zeus popped back home and chased Scylla off. Netta just hoped that the reporter didn't have any treats with which to bribe the familiar. Maven slowly relaxed, then looked at Netta over her glasses.

"Danny's looking pretty good these days."

Netta just shook her head, but Maven pushed on.

"He's been married to a witch once before. I'm sure that he wouldn't object to being married to another one. Especially since that adorable little girl of his possesses some amazing talents.

"She is a *doll*. I've worked with her a time or two. I let Danny know that I was aware of his wife's and his daughter's abilities."

Netta simply looked at Maven. She knew where the old witch was going with this conversation.

"Ayla would thrive if she had another witch in her life full-time," Maven said.

Netta groaned loudly.

"Please Maven. We were once good friends, but we've both changed since then."

"He's a handsome, single father with a magical little

girl. And you can't lie to me. I saw the way you two were looking at each other.

"I know sparks when I see them," the elder witch grinned.

ELEVEN

Netta didn't have too many customers the next morning, so she nursed a cup of coffee while she read the morning paper. She was one of the few people who still enjoyed getting the printed version of the news.

Of course, Scylla had managed to place one of her stories on the front page. She started out with the facts about Kevin's murder. However, true to Scylla form, she couldn't resist putting a little sensationalism in her article.

July Donovan, a maid at one of the Credo family hotels, was quoted by Scylla as saying that she didn't care who or what killed Kevin. She was just glad that he was gone. He would lurk in some of the rooms that he knew she still had to clean. Then, when she went in to do her job, he would jump out of the dark and grab her in a most unwelcome manner.

"It happened all the time and I was just sick and tired of it. I complained to my boss, but she told me to 'just deal with it.' Kevin's father said the same thing. I tried getting an attorney, but these guys are just too powerful, and I couldn't get anyone to help me," July said. "I don't have the money to try to hire some big-name lawyer from a different town.

"I felt trapped. There was no way out for me. So, all I can say to the person who killed Kevin Credo is thank you. I appreciate you."

Netta knew that people who felt cornered could do drastic things. She was sure that July would be able to find the instructions and ingredients to make the ricin gas. According to July's complaint, she would have the opportunity to administer it. She definitely had the motive.

After finishing her coffee and newspaper, Netta decided that she had better take care of some of her errands. She let Justine know what she was doing and headed out.

While she was at one of the local markets, she ran into July.

"Hey, I read your story about what was going on. I'm sorry that you went through all of that," Netta said.

"Thanks, I appreciate that. You are sweet. I'm just glad that the nightmare is over. I dreaded going to work every day, because I knew that Kevin Jr. would be there and if I wanted a job, I had to 'deal with it,'" July said.

"Why didn't you get another job?" Netta asked.

"Because that hotel paid twice as much as any other job in town. I couldn't afford to go somewhere else," July said. "But whoever killed Kevin did me a huge favor."

"I guess he or she did," Netta said.

"Do you think the killer could be a woman?" July asked, her eyes opened wide.

"Anything is possible," Netta said. "So, what are you going to do now?"

"Kevin's father paid me a quarter of a million dollars to not sue his hotel and leave town. I probably could have gotten more, but I just want to be done with this place and move on and get a fresh start."

"That makes sense," Netta said sympathetically.

They spoke for a few more minutes, and then Netta grabbed the items she needed and headed to the checkout to pay for them.

Janie, who owned the shop, was at the register.

"I saw you talking to July," Janie said.

Netta nodded, not wanting to say too much, because Janie was a notorious gossip. She knew everything about everybody, including how many times you blew your nose at night.

"That girl ain't got no troubles that she don't bring on herself," said Janie in a sassy voice. "She flirts with rich men, thinkin' that she's cute enough to catch her one. They want something from her, but they don't wanna pay for it with a ring.

"Then, when things don't work out the way that she planned it, she gets mad and complains that they were sexually harassing her."

Netta nodded, taking in the information. Being spurned by someone certainly is a motive for murder. As the old saying goes about a woman scorned...

Once Netta got home, she made notes in her journal. The rest of the day flew by, as she gave a diving lesson and made plans to wow the documentary directors when they showed up.

She was plenty tired at the end of the day, and decided to go to bed early.

But something woke her in the middle of the night. On the beach near the inn, she saw a series of weird flashing lights. The lights bobbed up and down, as though someone held them and waved them in a signal pattern. At least one of the lights was red.

She couldn't tell whether the lights were from flashlights or if a boat had come up on the beach right next to her property. Either way, she had to figure out what was going on.

Netta jumped up, got dressed, and grabbed her own flashlight.

Emily appeared as Netta left her bedroom and begged her not to go out, but Netta insisted. She had to figure out what was going on out there. She grabbed a baseball bat and headed toward the stairs. Sargasso accompanied her, as did Caspia's legs.

"You're too brave for your own good," the legs told her. "If you were smart, you'd call that cute cop guy that you're dating."

"You shush. I'm not dating anyone," Netta said, and continued heading toward the beach, ignoring her friends' admonitions. The cats padded after her. Emily hung behind, watching their progress from the inn's front porch.

The trio slowly approached the spot where Netta had seen the lights earlier. The area now appeared void of humans, but not of clues.

In the sand right in front of the inn, someone had drawn a skull and crossbones. Just like on a bottle of poison.

TWELVE

Danny was sound asleep when his phone rang. Having been a cop for several years, he was able to wake immediately when that familiar sound broke the peaceful silence of the night.

The first thing he heard was a lot of meowing, as though several cats were trying to tell him something at once. Unfortunately, he never learned to speak cat.

Then, Netta spoke, sounding calm, although he could tell that the calm was forced.

"Can you come to the inn as soon as possible? I've called 9-1-1, too, and they have sent some cops, but there is something that I think you need to see," Netta explained, her voice tight.

"What is it?" Danny asked, even as he jumped out of bed and started pulling on trousers.

"I'd rather you just see for yourself. But you need to hurry, before it's gone," Netta urged. "I don't know what it means, but it can't be good."

He promised Netta that he would be there very shortly,

and hung up. He felt grateful that he'd developed a talent for simultaneously getting dressed and juggling a phone.

Danny called his sister, who hurried over to stay with Ayla while he was gone. Then, grabbing his gun and badge, he headed to the inn, lights and sirens blaring.

He stopped short when he saw the symbol drawn in the sand. He knew exactly what that meant. Someone thought that Netta was getting too close to the investigation.

It was a direct threat.

"Who have you been talking to lately?" he asked Netta.

"The only person I've spoken to besides Marliss is July Donovan. I'm pretty sure that she didn't have anything to do with this drawing, especially since I didn't ask her any questions about the investigation. We spoke about her newspaper interview, and she told me the circumstances surrounding her statements. She said that Kevin's father had given her a lot of money so she could leave town. She was very happy about that," Netta answered.

"Well, it's obvious that someone thinks that you know more about the situation than you really do," Danny said.

Netta shrugged her shoulders.

"I have no idea. I didn't even seek July out, I ran into her at Janie's market. Besides talking to Marliss with you, I've just done the same things I've always done – run my inn and give scuba diving lessons. I haven't done anything to make anyone suspicious."

"Someone is worried about what they think you might have seen or heard. I suggest you quit talking about the situation entirely. Don't ask questions, don't talk to anyone who knew Kevin or had a problem with him, and don't answer any questions. You don't know who might be probing you for information," Danny said.

Netta drew herself up tall and stared at Danny.

"First, you *asked* for my assistance. You pointed out that I had an obligation to help in any way that I could or my town and my neighbors could suffer consequences. You asked, and you shall receive.

"Second, most of the people in town knew Kevin, and half of those had issues with him. He was not one of our more upstanding citizens.

"Third, I haven't answered any questions, because I have no answers. But if someone wants to come to me and talk about what they know about the case, how they knew Kevin, or any possible beefs they might have had with him, I'm going to listen," Netta said, her voice freezing cold.

She did not appreciate being ordered about, especially by someone who was a virtual stranger to her now.

Sargasso and Caspia both mewed loudly as though they were rooting her on. Emily simply gasped from the Inn's front porch and hung her head.

Danny looked around as though he had heard the gasp and was trying to figure out where it came from.

Emily covered her mouth and giggled. The sound really seemed to make Danny anxious. Then, he chalked it up to the night air making noises and shook it off.

He took out his phone to take pictures of the inscribed warning. It would likely disappear soon with waves or wind, and he wanted to make sure that he could examine every bit of it later. While he took pictures, Netta kept talking.

"Besides, you have no idea that this warning is really about the case. It could have been a bunch of teenagers or drunk people playing out here. There are all kinds of people who love legends about pirates.

"And while this symbol is on poison bottles, it is also on the Jolly Roger. This might be pirate fan art," Netta said, trying to sound reasonable.

"Why would they pick this exact spot to play pirate?" Danny asked.

"It could just be a coincidence. They could have been on a party barge, got off at the docks, and were walking back to their hotel when inspiration hit," Netta said.

The more she attempted to explain the situation, the more she regretted calling Danny. She was making a mountain out of a molehill. She figured that Kevin's death had her a little more rattled than she cared to admit.

"I don't believe in coincidences," Danny said. "In police business, coincidences are either clues or warnings – sometimes both."

"I think I just overreacted," Netta protested.

Shaking his head, he walked around the large symbol to see if there were any hidden messages that he could glimpse from the other side.

Just then, a huge gust of air caught the sand on the beach and lifted the drawing up whole. It whirled it about in a circle, twirled over to Netta and engulfed her.

Then, just as suddenly as it had started, the makeshift tornado exploded, spraying sand in a million different directions. Then the beach fell still again.

The symbol had disappeared in a most inexplicable way.

THIRTEEN

Netta went back to bed after everyone left, although it was almost time to get up again. She stared at the ceiling for a while, unable to fall back asleep.

She was angry.

If someone thought that they could scare her away by drawing pictures in the sand, they were dead wrong – no pun intended.

Whoever was doing this had essentially attacked her town and threatened her people. They had also threatened her business. If there was something that she could do to stop it, she would do it. She wasn't about to just sit by if there was any way she could help.

She managed to get about 90 minutes of sleep before her alarm went off. It was the first time in a long time she had experienced a violent urge to throw something across the room. Making sure that she didn't use any additional force, she clicked off the annoying beeper and got ready for the day.

No sooner had she made it downstairs when a huge

group of people came bustling in. The documentary directors and their crew had shown up earlier than expected. They were scheduled for later that afternoon.

Luckily, Netta had a couple of unoccupied rooms, so everyone was able to stow their luggage and gear. Justine put out saucers and refilled coffee cups like a pro. Soon the film folks were happily relaxing, while the witches took care of their departing guests.

When Netta looked up from their final check-out, one of the directors waved her over to the film group.

"We would like to go out a little deeper than you normally take your students," he said. "We would like to see coral reefs and wildlife that aren't found in shallower waters."

Netta nodded.

"I believe I can line up the boat I usually used to take out my more experienced divers." She hurriedly called the dock. Yes, her normal rental was available.

She felt grateful, because she was very familiar with the boat and how to operate it, so she wouldn't look like a fool trying to figure out a whole new craft.

Netta grabbed her gear out of the storage area, as well as some spare equipment. A diver never knew what kind of emergency situations might arise in the water.

When they got to the spot where they were going to dive, each person checked their own equipment, as per protocol. Everyone's was fine, except for Netta's.

Someone had cut her airlines.

The cuts were tiny and hard to detect, but her experienced eye picked them out immediately. Had she entered deep water with these tanks, they could have been deadly.

Shaken, she told the others to go on without her, she would be there in a minute. She didn't want to alarm anyone and blow this once-in-a-lifetime opportunity. She carefully checked the set of backup equipment. It appeared intact. She donned it and then joined the others.

The crew oohed and aahed over the scenery. The location manager asked her to demonstrate how she would instruct more experienced students, using them as stand-ins.

Completely calm, as she was now in her element, Netta showed them some of the dangers that lurked below in the waters and how to avoid them. She showed them how to react during various emergency situations.

The director and director of photography both complimented her on her technique, and said she was one of the best instructors that they had interviewed.

After a very satisfying morning, Netta served the crew the lasagna that Justine had brought in for the guests, and then the special desserts she had ordered from Victor's.

They loved the food, too.

Whew! Today is going well!

"We were wondering if you could show us around this afternoon?" the location manager asked.

"I have a better idea. My handyman has a carriage and some horses that he uses for tours. He knows the history of this town better than anyone else around. I think he knows more than the people who run the library and the town museum. His family helped found *Siren Key*."

She made the arrangements for Johnny to give the crew a tour, and then heaved a sigh of relief as the group disappeared around the bend in the guide's two-horse carriage.

But her relief was short-lived. She dreaded the phone call she had to make, because she knew that Danny was just going to give her a hard time. But she couldn't delay any longer.

She told Danny about the attempt to sabotage her air tanks. He, of course, lost no time rushing over with the forensics team.

They checked for fingerprints and any DNA evidence that the saboteur might have left behind but didn't find much. They took the items with them to examine them in the town's small but mighty lab.

"Netta, you need to make sure that everyone knows that you have nothing to do with this investigation," Danny said, starting the dreaded lecture.

"I haven't investigated anything," Netta protested. "What should I do, make a public announcement and say that while my client found the body, I don't know anything about the case so leave me alone?"

"That actually sounds like a great plan," Danny said. "I'm worried about you. I don't want to see you getting hurt because I asked you for help."

"No one knows you asked for my help except the cats," Netta said. "And while they are very clever, they aren't able to hold a knife and damage air hoses.

"The best way to ensure my safety is for you and I to get our buns out there and catch the bad guys."

Danny heaved a huge sigh in frustration.

"You are impossible, do you know that?" he asked.

"I've been told that a time or two," Netta answered.

Danny dropped an impulsive kiss on her cheek. Then he left.

Netta felt stunned.

And instead of thinking about warnings, sabotage, and murder, she could only think of the kiss.

FOURTEEN

D anny knew that he should keep his feelings separate from his work, but he was genuinely worried about Netta.

She'd blown the warning symbol off as a drunken prank. But cutting her air hoses was no joke. It was a serious threat to her life.

He felt guilty for asking her to help with the investigation, although at the time, he hadn't known what else to do. No one had even wanted to tell him their names, and it had been clear he wasn't going to get anywhere without local expertise.

While he waited on subpoenas for Marliss' airline ticket information, he decided to check out July. He agreed with Netta that he didn't think that she was responsible for killing Kevin, leaving the warning for Netta, or messing up Netta's equipment. But he wasn't going to leave anything to chance.

The word around the station was that July had made multiple claims of sexual harassment against a lot of men, which was the real reason that no attorney would work for her. She was the proverbial 'boy who cried wolf', and no one believed her cries any more.

Danny called Kevin Credo, Sr., the victim's dad, and asked him about July.

Credo sighed heavily through the phone.

"That woman has been a pain since she was hired. I don't really want to talk about her. However, you can call my attorney, Craig Collins. I will instruct him to tell you everything that you want to know."

Danny thanked the senior Credo for his time and hung up. After waiting about a half hour so Credo and Collins could talk, during which time he let his mind wander over the case, he dialed the attorney.

The attorney verified what Netta had learned from July and Janie, with a few additions.

"July hit on Kevin, and they had a one-night stand. But Kevin decided that July didn't put out what she was advertising and ended it. That was all there was to it.

"He could have practically any woman he wanted, given his fortune, so he told me that July wasn't worth his time or effort.

"She didn't take being rejected well and had begun hinting that she intended to accuse him of sexual harassment. To shut her up, Kevin started a lawsuit for harassment and slander."

"That could be a motive for murder," Danny said, more to himself than to the attorney.

"It is, but in my opinion, she's more of a con artist than a murderer," Craig answered. "And not a very skilled con artist at that.

"However, this time she at least got a little bit of what she was looking for. Mr. Credo offered her a large sum of money to leave town and not come back. She had to sign a contract that she would leave once she received the money, and she could not make any further accusations against Kevin Jr., or she would have to pay back every penny of the settlement with interest."

"Do you expect her to abide by that?" Danny asked.

"I do. She'll take the money and go to another town and resume her cons there. She'll harass other people into paying her to go away," Craig said, then chuckled dryly. "She ran out of rich men to scam here."

"You make her sound like she lacks strong moral character," Danny said.

"Bingo," Craig answered.

Danny thanked him for his time and hung up. He looked at his notes. And out of the blue, felt a sudden, irresistible urge to see Netta.

She smiled shyly at him when he walked into the inn. She grabbed a couple cups of coffee and sat down with him at one of the back tables.

"How's it going?" she asked.

"Okay. I just wanted to ask you how well you knew July," Danny said. Netta considered.

"Not at all, really. She arrived in town about a year ago. I've never had a reason to develop a relationship with her. I barely leave the inn, except to run errands once in a while. Why?"

Danny felt something rub against his leg. He looked down and saw Sargasso snuggling up to him and purring.

Suddenly, Danny needed to tell Netta everything he'd found out, although he knew that he shouldn't. He didn't want Netta getting more deeply involved than she already was.

But he couldn't seem to stop himself. He explained every little detail that he had learned from the attorney. By the time he was finished, he felt a little out of breath, as though the words had been forcibly expelled from his body.

I can't resist because I find her so attractive.

But that thought didn't make sense, because in the past, he had talked to other attractive women about cases without feeling the urge to spill his guts like this.

She must have put some kind of spell on me.

That thought jolted him. He knew that his wife had been a witch and could sometimes read other people's thoughts. So there would likely be other witches out there who could compel information out of people, like hypnotists.

He told himself those thoughts were absurd. Netta couldn't be a witch. He'd already had two witches in his life, and he considered it extremely unlikely that a third might come along.

"I really just wanted to come by and make sure that you're okay," he stammered. "I don't like the threats against you."

Netta stood up to walk him to the door.

Danny really wanted to ask her out to dinner but decided he'd better not. For her safety, he should wait until the case was solved. He didn't want to put her in any more danger than she was already in.

But as he left the inn, he wondered.

Was he in danger too? Of falling for his old flame?

FIFTEEN

The documentary film crew raved about everything in *Siren Key*. Johnny had been a great guide and had told them many entertaining tales about the history of their little town.

They had also gushed about Victor's desserts. The gold-flaked delicacies were very expensive, but if it would help Netta secure a spot in the documentary, they would have been worth the cost a hundred times over.

"Justine, I'm going to head over to Victor's and pick up some more sweets for our guests. Do you want anything?" Netta asked her best friend.

Justine shook her head.

"Nope. I'm lasagna-ed out. I've eaten enough to last me at least the next year. Thanks, though."

The first thing that Netta noticed when she walked into Victor's was that Knoll Curry, who had been a good friend of Kevin's and was known as a thug for hire, sat in a booth with Scylla.

Deciding that she might hear something interesting, she

decided to slip into the booth in front of them. Neither noticed her.

"To be honest, I think Kevin got involved with drugs," Knoll told Scylla.

"Everyone thinks that," Scylla said in her very annoying voice. "Do you have anything to say that I haven't already heard?"

"I know that he had been hanging out recently with Tony Barellas. The feds have been looking at him for a long time, trying to catch him running drugs between here and Colombia, and from here to Cuba. But Tony is way too smart to get caught," Knoll said.

"That really isn't all that interesting either," Scylla replied, sounding remarkably, even theatrically, bored.

"Well, this might be interesting," Knoll said. "I went to Kevin's house after the murder because he owed me money. I know he has a hidden shelf in his closet behind a fake wall.

"When I opened it, I saw packets of white powder, powders of two or three other colors, and liquids in jars and bottles. I didn't touch anything because I didn't want my fingerprints on stuff that might be drug-related.

"I sure as heck wouldn't sell meth or cocaine to kids just to get my money back. I do have morals, you know."

"Now *that* is interesting, Knoll," Scylla said. Netta could hear the reporter typing furiously on the tablet she always carried around with her.

"He must have done something to make the big guys mad at him, and they took him out for it," Knoll said, eagerly, as though he was trying to please the reporter.

"Can I quote you as an anonymous source?" she asked.

Knoll nodded.

"Yeah, but be careful about the anonymous part. I don't want anyone to come after me, you know."

"I can make that happen. I really appreciate the information. This will make for great headlines. If you remember anything else, call," Scylla said. Then, she gathered up her computer and purse and left, not looking around her to see if anyone had overheard the conversation, which was a good thing for Netta.

As she left, the kitchen doors flew open. Victor carried Netta's order out. He stopped by Knoll's booth first.

"I saw you talking to that reporter chick. What was that all about?" Victor asked. Netta thought that he sounded angry.

"We were just talking about Kevin. She came to see me because she knew we were friends. I told her that I thought he was selling drugs and probably got whacked by the bigshot dealers," Knoll said.

"I agree. Or he could have been killed by Scylla just so she could get some ratings. Other than that, the only thing that goes on around here is when there is a fight at the bar or someone gets drunk and shoots out the stop signs," said Victor dryly.

Knoll laughed.

"That ratings thing. I heard Scylla was doing some illegal stuff in Tampa."

"Everyone's heard that," Victor said. "I have product for you to deliver. It's in the back and it's marked. Make sure you get payment before you hand it over. Otherwise, people will say that their order was messed up and refuse to pay me."

"Yes, sir," Knoll said, sliding out of his booth.

As he headed toward the kitchen, Netta slipped out of her booth, too. Victor narrowed his eyes at her.

"I didn't see you there. I figured you'd be waiting at the front, like normal," Victor said.

Netta had a feeling he was lying and had known that she was there the entire time, but she played along anyway.

"I was just tired and needed a second to think," she improvised. "You run a busy place. People are always coming and going and they want to say hello.

"I figured if I sat here, I could just stare off into space and daydream about the possibility of getting a spot on this documentary. They only have room for five, and I'm in the top eight candidates. I'm hoping to bribe them with your delicious sweets." Netta gushed as best she could, hoping that he would find her story flattering enough to let any suspicions go.

"Thank you for the compliment," Victor said, handing her the boxes.

"You know, if I get on the documentary, there is a good chance that they will mention your restaurant, too. You and your desserts will be famous worldwide. Then, you'll have to make goodies twenty-four hours a day just to keep up with the rush."

"That would certainly be something," Victor said.

She bid him goodbye and noticed that he watched her walk to Ginger to pay for the food. Surely, he wasn't 'policing' her payment? No, she decided he was probably just calculating all of the money he would be raking in if he was mentioned in the documentary.

Netta drove by the police station to tell Danny what she had overheard about the secret closet in Kevin's house. Danny thanked her for the tip and told her to stay safe.

She waved goodbye and took off, thinking about her next move.

And all the trouble she was about to cause.

SIXTEEN

Netta thought about Scylla. The conversation she'd overheard between Knoll and Victor was the second time someone mentioned that Scylla had instigated crime to get a scoop.

She wondered what Scylla had to say about the situation.

Emily, the kitten familiars, and Justine all told her that visiting Scylla was a terrible idea and that she should just let Danny handle the situation.

"It is just a rumor," Netta said. "I can't send him on a wild goose chase, stealing time from leads that might actually pan out. Besides, he did ask for my help, so he shall receive my help, even if all I do is eliminate a suspect."

"He also *rescinded* his request for help," Justine said.

"Only because he's worried about me. The faster the killer is caught, the less Danny has to worry about," Netta said. She waved goodbye and left before anyone else could throw in an unsolicited opinion.

She walked into the news station and asked for Scylla.

"Netta. Oh my gosh. It is so good to see you. I've wanted to talk to you for so long," Scylla gushed.

"I've heard something about the case. I was hoping that you could help me," Netta said.

"I would love to. Come back to my office with me," Scylla cooed.

Scylla sat behind her desk, her fingers ready at the keyboard, ready to type in whatever juicy information Netta had for her.

"I've heard from two different sources that you were fired in Tampa for staging crime scenes so that you could get the scoop. There is some speculation that you might have killed Kevin for the same reason," Netta said, deciding that being direct was the best way to get an honest reaction out of Scylla.

All of the color drained out of Scylla's face. Then, it flushed red with anger.

"That is *not* the reason that I left Tampa. I left because I was tired of being sexually harassed by the manager there. He thought that I should be his girlfriend because I was the star of the show and prettier than everyone else. He wouldn't take no for an answer," Scylla protested.

"What was this manager's name?" Netta asked. "Why didn't you take him to court? Everyone is winning lawsuits for sexual harassment these days."

"Bill Cummings. And I might have won a court settlement, but it would have ended my career. No one would have hired me after that. I would have built up a reputation just like that July woman," Scylla said, her voice rising in fury.

"I can't believe that rumor got started here. I wouldn't even kill a spider, let alone a human being, even if he was a scumbag.

"Besides, when Kevin was killed I was in a meeting with the editors. They were trying to find ways to bring in younger readers."

In her anger, Scylla forgot to use her valley girl accent, and instead sounded like a true angry, Southern woman.

Netta nodded.

"Okay. The next time I hear the rumor, I will defend you. We might not be friends, but I don't like untrue gossip being spread around. It just isn't nice."

"Thank you," Scylla said, looking at Netta suspiciously.

"I'll see you later," Netta said, and left. Once outside the station, she called Danny and told him what she'd learned.

"I told you to back off of the investigation! Someone thinks you know things, so you need to distance yourself, Netta!"

"But will you check out Scylla's alibi?"

Danny sighed so heavily his lungs rattled.

"Yes, Netta. I will check out Scylla's alibi."

Netta disconnected, and promptly made a beeline for Scylla's house. She didn't think Scylla had anything to do with the murder, but she wanted to know if she could find files on the case.

Scylla did seem to be truly interested in investigating Kevin's bizarre death, whether it was because she was a good reporter, she wanted the ratings, or she was simply nosy.

Netta slipped in the back door, which Scylla had left unlocked. She found Scylla's office and hit pay dirt.

Apparently, Scylla had been investigating allegations that someone in or near *Siren Key* was manufacturing illegal drugs and chemical weapons. That made sense, sadly, since coastal areas had long been prime locations for those types of activities, given their easy access to water transport.

Scylla had interviewed Marliss, and Netta read her notes from their conversation. It appeared that Marliss' father had been one of the scientists creating the aforementioned chemical weapons, and one day, Daddy turned up shot to death.

Marliss had been overcome with grief. She and her father were very close, and Marliss said that she felt completely lost in the world without him.

Kevin had been taking a walk in the park when he saw Marliss sitting on a bench just staring at the sky, trying to figure out what to do with her life. He sat down and spoke with her.

Scylla quoted Marliss.

"It must have made him laugh that he was comforting the daughter of the man he had killed. Kevin never said he executed Daddy, but I *know* it was him."

It would appear that Marliss was on to something. Netta didn't know how Scylla had gotten the information, but the file contained some of Kevin's bank statements.

The day after Marliss' father had been murdered, Kevin had deposited a large sum of money into his bank account. While it didn't prove anything, it certainly was suggestive.

Netta took out her phone and started taking pictures of Scylla's notes. Danny would yell at her, but he would also have to thank her for finding such a rich vein of information.

Netta was so engrossed in what she was doing that she hadn't paid attention to her surroundings. She started when she heard a key turn in the front door lock.

Her heart thundered in her chest and she couldn't seem to inhale.

The doorknob started to turn. Then, she heard Scylla exclaim in seeming delight.

"What a beautiful little kitten! Listen to you purr. What soft fur you have!"

Sargasso? What was he doing here?

The kitten must have apparated the split-second before Scylla entered her home.

Netta looked around. She had to escape while Scylla was distracted.

SEVENTEEN

etta padded silently to the back of the house. Luckily, Scylla had a rear door. She hurriedly opened it and headed out, shutting it quietly behind her just as Scylla opened the front door.

Netta owed Sargasso a huge thanks.

What if Scylla wants to keep him as a pet? She chuckled. *What will he do then?*

But she knew better than to worry. Sargasso was as devious as he was adorable.

She headed back to the inn, and after suffering through everyone chastising her for breaking into Scylla's house and almost getting caught, she decided that she needed to bite the bullet and tell Danny what she had learned.

Danny's cell rang as he sat in his office looking over his notes, trying to figure out where to go next with the investigation.

"I did something that is going to make you a little mad, but good came out of it, so you can't yell at me," Netta said in his ear.

Danny sighed heavily again—he seemed to do that a lot these days—and asked her what she did.

"First, I want to know if you checked out Scylla's alibi," Netta said.

"I shouldn't tell you anything," Danny said. "You are not an investigator."

"If you don't tell, I won't tell," Netta teased.

"Fine. Actually, I don't see the harm in updating you. Scylla was telling the truth. She was in a meeting with her editors from seven in the morning until noon. She could not have killed Kevin – unless she got someone to do it for her," Danny said. "Now spill."

Netta took a deep breath for courage.

"After I visited Scylla at her office, I decided to visit her house."

"You knew she wasn't home," Danny said, his tone showing that he clearly didn't like where this story was going.

"That's why I went. Anyway..." Netta hurriedly continued before Danny could break in. "I found out some interesting information. Kevin was definitely into something dirty, all the way up to his eyeballs." She summarized what she'd learned, and said that she would send the pictures she took to him.

"Thanks for the information, but you cannot go around breaking into people's houses! That is called breaking and entering, and that is against the law! If you were anyone else, I would arrest you," Danny said.

"It's your fault," Netta countered. "You're the one who told me I should get involved in the investigation. I was happy just running my inn and swimming with the sharks," she said, amusement evident in her voice.

Danny heaved yet another huge sigh.

"Thank you for the information. Don't do it again."

"Let me know what you find out," Netta said, and then hung up before Danny tried to make her promise not to break into any more houses.

Danny shook his head. It seems that he created a monster. But Netta was right. Looking through Kevin's financial records was an important step in investigating his death.

He saw that the bank hadn't followed through on the subpoena yet, so he called. The manager sounded very nervous, but promised that he would send a courier over with the information immediately.

Danny wondered what had the manager rattled. Maybe he was worried about getting in trouble for not complying with the subpoena?

The courier arrived within ten minutes. Danny thanked him and retreated to his office, looking through the documents.

Scylla was right to be suspicious of the murder victim.

According to the statements, Kevin had four different bank accounts. The day after Marliss' father had been killed, Kevin had made a nine-thousand-dollar deposit into three of them. He made the same deposits the following day. The amounts were just under the ten-thousand-dollar mark which the banks would have legally been forced to report to the IRS.

After that, he made several large deposits into each of the three accounts every month, just under the magical $10,000. They were cash deposits, which made them untraceable.

What was Kevin up to? Whatever it was had gotten him killed...

Kevin also had a fourth account which was almost

empty. That must have been the one from which he paid Marliss.

He had plenty of money to pay child support with. He just didn't want to.

What a jerk.

Danny sat back in his chair wondering how he could trace the money. He had tried to trace Kevin's steps, but it was almost like he had walked out of Netta's bar and totally disappeared until he was found dead a few hours later.

He had also tried to figure out where Kevin spent his days and nights. But again, it seemed that he had disappeared for long periods of time and no one knew his whereabouts.

The secret panel in Kevin's closet had yielded no clues, much to the police team's disappointment. If Knoll had been telling the truth, the drugs, or whatever he saw, weren't there anymore.

Danny felt as though he was walking around in circles – working hard, but not going anywhere.

His phone rang. He hoped that this would be something that could jump start the investigation.

"Hey Danny, I have some more info for you," Drake said.

"I'm listening."

"I've had experts run additional tests. That ricin gas that was used on Kevin was weapons-grade. It was made to be put into aerosol cans which could be used on a large number of people. A terrorist could spray it in a train car, bus station, or even in a busy restaurant. There would be a lot of dead people," Drake said.

"I've notified Homeland Security, so if you are going to solve this, you might hurry up. Otherwise, the feds are probably going to take your case away from you."

"Thanks for the information and the warning," Danny said.

After hanging up, he thought about what this would mean for the town and everyone in it. If the feds suddenly infiltrated *Siren Key*, everyone would know. That could make the terrorist cell get antsy and take out civilians.

He called Netta.

"Look, I know you want to help. But the ricin gas that killed Kevin was weapons-grade. These people mean business. Please walk away from this," Danny pleaded.

"I can't. This is my town and these are my people," she said. "Be safe, Danny."

She hung up before he could reply.

EIGHTEEN

Netta, who used to be able to fall asleep as soon as her head hit the pillow, struggled, once again to drop off.

This is getting to be a very annoying trend.

Finally, she dozed, tossing and turning, until she was completely tangled up in her sheets.

Many minutes later, she had just fallen into a deep sleep when bright lights shone through her bedroom window and straight into her face, like someone hit her with a spotlight. She jumped out of bed and ran to the window.

This time, she could see the outline of a boat in the harbor. The craft had finally turned its lights off, but there were people on the shore loading things onto the boat, and they all had flashlights.

She ran out to see what was going on, being careful to stay in the shadows. Sargasso and a small white kitten face followed her out.

Netta saw the mysterious crew load wooden crates of different sizes onto the boat. Everyone handled the boxes gingerly, as though they were full of bombs poised to explode.

A tall man stood off to one side. He looked like he was directing the complex choreography. He had a clipboard and seemed to be making notes of the boxes that went on board. Netta wished she could get her hands on that clipboard. It could tell her everything that she needed to know.

The supervisor had shoulder-length curly hair, a square chin, and a long nose. Netta thought that he looked like Knoll, but she couldn't be sure since it was so dark out.

After about ten minutes, all the boxes were loaded, and the boat slid silently back into the water, only turning on its lights when it was further out. A couple of the men gathered around the supervisor and conferred in hushed whispers.

Netta cautiously turned to go back inside. However, she kicked a small can that a careless tourist had dropped in front of the inn. The men suddenly stopped talking and all but one scattered. The man that Netta thought was Knoll walked toward her, shining his flashlight exactly where Netta had been standing a few seconds earlier.

As he approached, Sargasso let out a loud screech that sounded like an angry wildcat. He darted right in front of Knoll.

The man laughed.

"I guess we're all jumpy. We were scared away by a freaking cat."

Then, he headed back into the darkness and Netta gratefully slipped inside the inn, only to encounter a livid kitten.

"You need to stop that," Sargasso said. "That is the second time that I've had to save your tushy. I might not be around the next time you're in danger."

"You're always around. That's what I pay you for," Netta said.

"Then I need a raise," Sargasso growled.

She called Danny and told her what she saw. He said he would send some people over to investigate.

"Thank you for the information and for not going closer to see what exactly was going on. *Now stop investigating. Next time, just call me,*" Danny chastised.

"That's what I tried to tell her," Emily said, giggling because she knew he couldn't hear her.

Both Emily and Netta were surprised by his next question.

"What was that noise? It sounded like a whoosh of wind. Are you outside?"

"No, it must be my cell service," Netta quickly answered, frowning at Emily. "I'm going back to bed."

The next day, Netta didn't really know what to do, so she decided that she would check on Marliss' alibi. She was sure that Danny had already done so, but he wouldn't give her the information and she wanted to know.

Diana, who owned the diner, greeted her.

"I'm so glad you're here. I have a bit of an emergency," she said.

"What did you lose this time?" Netta asked, smiling, used to Diana's 'emergencies'. Diana was the only mundane human in town who knew Netta's true identity and her talent.

"My glasses," Diana answered, looking a little embarrassed.

"Where did you have them last?"

Diana pointed to the register. Netta walked over and touched the machine. She saw a picture of where the glasses were. They had been picked up with a plate, coffee cup, and utensils, and taken to the back to be washed.

"Oh, that naughty bus boy," Diana said. She retrieved the wayward specs and fretted while she cleaned the lenses.

"The dishwasher would have brought them back," Netta said, confidently.

After the glasses were set perfectly on Diana's pert nose, she studied Netta.

"What can I do for you my dear? Although you always seem to show up when I need you, I'm sure you didn't come here just to find my glasses," Diana said.

"I was wondering if Marliss was here," Netta asked.

"She hasn't stopped in for a couple of days. She said that she was taking her baby and leaving, because it was too dangerous around here. And before you ask, she didn't say where she was going."

"I was wondering if she was working at the time that Kevin was killed," Netta asked.

"I remember that day. She came in right after the news broke. She was angry at him, and she felt bad for making a mess at the inn by throwing coffee around," Diana said.

She grabbed the timecards from her office and showed Netta the one that tracked Marliss' hours. Just as Netta thought. Marliss may not have been fond of her ex-whatever, but she couldn't have killed him.

"I'm down a waitress. Do you need an extra job?" Diana asked.

"Sorry, Diana. I have my hands full," Netta answered.

"My loss," Diana smiled. Netta kissed the old woman's cheek and headed out.

Netta didn't know whether to be happy or sad that Marliss wasn't the killer. She felt happy because she didn't want the single mother, who doted on her son, to be taken away from him.

But she also felt sad because Diana's information left her with no suspects and no leads.

NINETEEN

At the end of the day, Danny found himself wandering over to Netta's inn without even thinking about it. He wasn't sure what he was going to say to her, although the idea of asking her out for dinner still bounced around his brain, even if his good sense told him to wait until the case was resolved.

He was honest enough to admit that he just wanted to see her.

His phone started vibrating in his pocket as he stepped onto the inn's porch. He groaned when he saw that it was from the police department.

"Detective Sussex," he answered.

"Hey, this is Ken from dispatch. I have a call that I think you should take, it might be related to your case."

"Okay, forward it, please," Danny said.

"Detective Sussex," he answered.

"Hello, Detective. This is Lieutenant Jennifer Bradshaw of the United States Coast Guard," came a soft voice. "We were patrolling the area when we found a boat that appeared to drift aimlessly. There were two deceased persons on board that died a couple of hours before our arrival.

"Our medic, who has trained in chemical weaponry, said that the victims looked like they had been exposed to ricin gas via an aerosol can.

"I wanted to clue you in because we heard that you're working a case with a similar cause of death."

"Thank you. There has to be a connection because that would be too much of a coincidence. Can you have your investigators contact me if they get any new information? I will do the same on my end," Danny said.

"Absolutely. We need to get this thing cleared up before other people die," she said, and hung up.

Danny decided to let Netta know the latest development in hopes that if he told her the bad guys were upping their game, she might back away. He doubted it, but he had to take the chance. He didn't want anything bad to happen to her.

He stepped inside the inn.

Netta was shocked at his news.

"I wonder if those were the same guys I saw last night," she said.

"They probably were. You *must* step back from this, Netta. They are dangerous. Chances are excellent they aren't small-time thugs. They have access to weapons of mass destruction and appear to have no problems dispensing with people who get in their way."

"I'm not backing down but I'm not putting myself out there either. No one knows that I've been helping you," Netta repeated.

Danny growled, frustrated with her stubbornness. He opened his mouth to argue when his phone rang again.

"There is a cell phone under the cabana where Kevin's

body was found. You might want to check it out," a muffled voice said. Then the caller hung up.

Danny stared at his phone. Then he called the station, and arranged for two uniforms to meet him at Maven's cabana.

He told Netta to stay where she was, so naturally, she followed him to his car to grab evidence collection equipment, then over to Maven's shop.

As they approached, the elder witch hurried outside, curls rioting all over her head.

"What in the name of the rocks and trees are you doing snooping around my place?" she asked, staring pointedly at Danny.

"We received a tip that we'd find a lost cell phone near here that's connected to my case," Danny said.

Maven groaned.

"I just succeeded in driving away the last batch of nosy tourists," she said.

"How many of them became frogs?" Netta whispered to her mentor.

Maven glared at her, although Netta could see that her lips curled up in a smile.

"I ain't telling you, you impudent witch," she murmured back.

Danny hunted around under the cabana, pushing aside bladderwrack, bits of shell, sea glass, and other oceanic detritus. He saw the phone. He pulled on gloves and picked it up.

When the uniforms arrived, Danny handed them the phone, sealed into an evidence bag.

"Get this to the lab immediately. Ask them to check for fingerprints or DNA. Once forensics has finished, ask them to drop this on my desk so I can check out the contents," Danny instructed.

"Yes sir," said the woman officer, and they strode off.

Danny looked around for further clues that might tell him who placed the phone there.

"It has to be a plant," he muttered to himself. "There was no way that we would have missed it the day Danny was killed."

"I agree," Netta said, watching him work. She predicted that his efforts would end in frustration. The problem was obvious. Around Maven's cabana, she could clearly see how hundreds of footprints, going in every direction, roiled the white sand.

There was no way to follow any particular set of prints.

"This is very frustrating," Danny said.

"That's why you need my help. I've found you a couple of clues already. You need me," Netta said, smugly.

"You have been a great help," he said. "I can't argue with that. However, this case is just getting too dangerous for you. I really need you to back out, because I don't want to see anything happen to you. These people mean business."

Netta crossed her arms.

"I mean business, too."

Danny just shook his head. He would have better luck arguing with a brick wall.

"I'm heading back to the office. It shouldn't take them too long to search for evidence," he told her.

"Will you tell me if you find anything important?" Netta asked.

"No," Danny said. "Your liaison position has been cut, effective immediately. I'll see you later."

Danny got into his car and drove to the station. He had a sneaking suspicion that he would be seeing Netta sooner rather than later. She would *have* to know what was on that phone and she would chew on him like a bulldog on a bone until she found out.

TWENTY

etta had an afternoon lesson that day, so her trip to the police department would have to be put off. Her student was a ten-year-old, so her tutelage would only last an hour.

As always, once Netta got into the water, time flew by. The little girl had been terrified at first, as this was her first time going under wearing a tank and the attendant gear. However, she quickly adjusted, as the youngest students often did. Soon, Netta knew she would be diving into the water from a boat instead of the long pier near the inn's wash house.

When they came out of the water, Netta's heart dropped. There were a couple of policemen near the cabana talking to Maven. Then, she realized that they were probably following up on the cellphone discovery, and asking Maven what she'd seen and heard.

Netta reflected. Ever since Kevin's dead body had greeted her and her client, she was almost afraid to come out of the water, because she never knew what she might find.

The case is starting to get to me. Maybe I should lay off.

"Should" was the operative, and futile, word. Netta knew that she *should*, but that she wouldn't.

Her little student ran off to her mother, chirping happily about the exciting things they saw and the "cool" things she learned today.

"Miss Netta said I was going to be a pro in no time," the little girl proclaimed.

Smiling, Netta walked over to the policemen. They greeted her, and confirmed it had been Kevin's phone that was found. They were trying to figure out when and how it got there.

"This case certainly has been a struggle," she said. "All kinds of crazy things going on."

When she returned to the inn, Justine was dealing with several guests and seemed frantic, so Netta jumped in to help.

Once they were caught up, Justine rubbed her tummy.

"I sure could use some fettuccini alfredo with spicy shrimp. I wonder where I could get such a delicious dish?"

"Talk about hints," Netta laughed. "Didn't you have a date or something? You asked for a little time off this evening."

"I cancelled. Drake and I chatted on the phone this morning and all he wanted to talk about were fifty million different ways that you could skin and gut fish," Justine said.

"That sounds creepy to me," Netta said. "Like a serial killer in training."

"You watch too many true crime movies. Go fetch me food, woman," Justine said.

"I thought I was the boss here," Netta said. "I'm supposed to give orders."

"Not a chance," Sargasso purred from the sunlit windowsill. "That's me."

Netta laughed, and after she changed from dive gear to clothes, she headed over to Victor's restaurant. She gave her order to Ginger for two spicy shrimp fettuccini alfredos, and cannolis for dessert. Then, she slid into a back booth.

Two voices drifted out from the kitchen. She wasn't paying attention at first, but Victor's resonant baritone was hard to miss.

"You have been doing a great job lately," Victor said. "You've really stepped up to the plate, organizing all of the deliveries, making sure that they get there on time and collecting the fees, as expected. There is another big delivery coming up."

"I'll take care of it, boss," Knoll said.

As they walked out of the kitchen, Netta saw Victor hand Knoll an impressive wad of cash. She guessed that Victor paid his favorite delivery boy under the table so Knoll could avoid taxes.

Victor glanced at her and frowned briefly before turning back to Knoll and saying something quietly. Then, Knoll left and Victor hurried over to her.

"Hey there, did someone get your order?" he asked Netta.

She nodded.

"Ginger did. I was just sitting here, waiting. I love giving lessons, but sometimes, they wear me out," Netta said, smiling pleasantly at Victor.

About that time, Ginger came over with the order. Victor took the check and said that it was on the house.

"That is very kind, but it really isn't necessary," Netta protested.

"Nonsense. You have sent me a lot of customers and

bought several of my gold-flaked desserts lately. It is my way of saying 'thank you,'" Victor said.

"Thank *you*. I appreciate it. That is sweet of you," she replied.

"You know, I do have a delivery service. Instead of coming all the way over here and waiting, you can just put in a call and we'll deliver it. I've hired Knoll and a couple other people to take care of my VIP clients. You certainly qualify as one of those.

"And Knoll has been doing a great job lately. He's going to be in charge of scheduling all of the deliveries," Victor said.

"That's terrific. I'm glad that he is doing so well," Netta said. "Especially so soon after Kevin died. I know they were close."

"Perhaps it helped him understand how delicate life is and that he needed to get himself together. We never know when it's going to be our turn," Victor said.

"Very true," Netta said, sliding out of the booth, ready to leave. She had never really liked talking to Victor, because he never knew when to stop. But she didn't want to be rude, either.

"Is there anything that you would like to see added to the menu?" he asked her as he walked her to the door. "I'm going to expand it. Plus, with business going so well, I was thinking about opening up a couple of restaurants in Orlando and Miami."

"That sounds amazing. I can't think of anything to add right now, but I'll ask Justine. She's your biggest fan."

"You give that sweet girl a hug for me," Victor said.

"I sure will. Thanks for dinner," Netta said, waving as she left. When she finally sat down in her car, she breathed a sigh of relief. She didn't think that she was ever going to get out of there.

She drove home thinking about Knoll and his deliveries.

Was he really getting himself together? Or was he just biding time until his next round of trouble?

TWENTY-ONE

Netta decided to stop by the station early the next morning, when she figured Danny would be getting in. She brought him some coffee and a cinnamon apple muffin.

As soon as he saw her, Danny figured that she had an ulterior motive for visiting, and he was right. As they talked about the clients that she had scheduled for the day, she kept eyeing the cell phone they'd found under Maven's cabana.

"We really need to get this case cleared up," Netta said. "It didn't do my heart any good to come out of the water yesterday and see cops near the cabana again. I doubt if it will do my business any good either. Do you think that we are getting close?" she asked.

"We could be," he said. He noticed that her attention was focused on Kevin's phone. He knew that she wanted to read the text messages, but he couldn't legally allow that.

"I'm going to refill my coffee, although the swill in the lounge isn't nearly as delicious as what you brought me,"

Danny said, and shot her a significant look before he strolled off.

As soon as he left, Netta grabbed the phone and headed straight for the text messages. Most of the latest were between July and Kevin.

I'm so sick of you harassing me. You make it seem as though I'm crazy, but I can't go anywhere without you grabbing me, she said.

You are accusing me of it, so I might as well do it, Kevin replied.

You will pay for making my life a living nightmare, she said.

Make one more step toward me, and I will go through with my plan for suing you for defamation of character. You can't prove your case but I can prove mine, he typed.

You'll regret that, was the last message on the phone from July.

Netta put the phone back where she found it and tried to look innocent when Danny came back in the room. Danny just smiled at her and shook his head.

"So, what are you going to do now?" Netta asked.

"I have a couple of weak leads, nothing that seems to be going anywhere," he said. "But I have to check them all out, because the one that I skip will be the one that breaks the case wide open."

Netta nodded.

"I've tried to call July, but I can't seem to get hold of her," Danny said.

"I could help with that," Netta said. "I'll casually ask around and put out some feelers. There couldn't be much danger in that," Netta said.

Danny looked at her for a minute as though he wanted to tell her no. However, two things stopped him. First, she was going to do it anyway. Second, she did have stronger ties to the community and was likely to get the information he needed a lot quicker than he could.

"Okay, but you come to me as soon as you get any information, or if you think that you are being followed, or if anything else hinky goes on," Danny told her.

"Is hinky illegal?" Netta asked, pretending that she was totally serious.

"In this case, hinky is illegal and seems to be very dangerous, especially where you're concerned," Danny answered, completely serious.

They chatted for a few more minutes and then Netta left to meet her next student.

Danny sat back in his chair and wondered how Netta and his daughter Ayla would get along. He figured they'd be a match made in heaven. They both had an uncanny way of knowing things and they both seem to have talents that other people didn't have.

Of course, he knew that Ayla had inherited her mother's witchy ways, but he didn't think that Netta could be a witch. That would just be too weirdly coincidental.

Netta just had really great instincts.

He thought that he would like to introduce the two of them, even if romance never bloomed between him and Netta.

Perhaps Netta could give his daughter diving lessons. He would have to caution Ayla to not make all of the underwater plants grow, because they would take over and destroy the delicate ecosystems.

On the other hand, maybe she could do some good by healing coral reefs. Then in the back of his mind, he remembered a teacher saying that corals were technically animals.

His thoughts flowed back to Netta. He hoped they

might stumble into romance after this mess was over. She was smart, kind, and one of the strongest women he knew. Everything that he wanted in a partner.

Danny's thoughts about Netta were interrupted by an officer coming into his office saying that he had a phone call.

When he answered, a muffled voice said, "July. 407-555-6152."

Then the call went dead.

Someone was trying very hard to put him onto July's tail. Too hard. Regardless of how angry July might have been at Kevin, Danny didn't believe she killed him. Especially since daddy dearest paid up.

And speaking of money, Danny figured July had received her payout and left town. But it couldn't hurt to call. He dialed the number the anonymous tipster had offered. July answered on the first ring.

"Hello?"

"Is this July Donovan?" Danny asked.

"Yes. And you are?" she asked.

"This is Detective Danny Sussex from the *Siren Key* Police Department. I was wondering if you could come in so we could talk about Kevin Credo," he said.

"No. I'm too busy for that. All you need to know is that I didn't kill him and I don't know who did. All of the issues I had with him are now resolved, and I am moving to North Carolina in two weeks, as soon as my apartment there is available. Please do not call me again."

Before Danny could say another word, she hung up.

TWENTY-TWO

Netta was cleaning her gear after her latest lesson and planning the rest of her day when her phone rang. Seeing that it was Danny, her heart beat just a little bit faster.

She reflected briefly that the passing years had done nothing but make him more handsome, which foiled her attempts to focus on anything but her rapidly-deepening feelings for him.

"Well, fancy hearing from you," Netta said.

"I called to order more coffee and muffins," Danny said. "I heard you deliver."

"Mmm, that was a once-in-a-lifetime opportunity. But our lovely Justine is always available should you drop in," Netta said.

"I might. However, I was actually calling about something else. I had an anonymous tip, from probably the same person that told me where to find Kevin's phone. The caller gave me July's new number.

"I phoned July, and she said she wouldn't come in but

that she didn't know anything about Kevin's murder and to never call her again."

Netta smiled.

"I think I know what this call is about. It really isn't about coffee and muffins. You want me to accidentally run into July and talk to her."

"Something along those lines," Danny said. "I really don't want you to be involved in the investigation, but I feel like I keep running into concrete barriers."

"No worries, I've got this. It can't hurt me because I don't think that July was involved," Netta said.

"I agree. And I'd really like to find out where she was when Kevin was killed," Danny said.

Netta walked into the inn. As expected, her favorite resident ghost popped up as she walked in.

"Hi all. Danny asked me to talk to July for him, since she won't give him the time of day," she said, and then looked at Emily. "I know you have the knack for knowing everyone's locations. Do you happen to know where July might be?"

"I do, actually. According to the schedule she normally keeps, she should be at the nail salon right about now," Emily said.

Netta groaned. She really didn't want to take time out of her busy day to get her nails done. But, if it could help solve this case, she would do it.

Just as Emily predicted, July sat in one of the chairs, chatting away as the manicurist filed her nails.

Netta slid into the chair next to her. The manicurist looked at her fingernails and then gave Netta a disgusted look. Netta shrugged. She had to admit that her nails were a mess. Her life burst with responsibilities, so her nails were not a priority.

July looked over and greeted Netta.

"It's been a long time, huh?" she asked.

"A while," Netta agreed, thinking that never qualified as a long time. "How have you been doing?"

"Great," July exclaimed. "I'm moving to North Carolina in two weeks. I'm so excited. I've bought a bunch of brand-new furniture and clothes. I'm leaving my old life completely behind."

"What are you going to do up there?" Netta asked her.

"I was thinking about opening up my own nail salon. I think that it would be a lot of fun," July said, enthusiastically.

"I'm worried about business here," Netta told her. "I'm afraid that all the rumors going around about Kevin's murder will scare off the tourists. Most of the town's money comes from tourism. My inn depends on visitors, and a lot of them want to take scuba diving tours."

July didn't say anything. Her friendly look had turned to one of suspicion.

Netta plowed on.

"I'm a little nervous now each time I return from a diving lesson. That's where I was when he was killed. I came out of the water, and bang! There was his body."

July rolled her eyes.

"So, that's why you're here. I had heard that you and Danny Boy had hooked up. You're fishing for information."

Netta tried to protest, but July wasn't having any of it.

"If you must know, I was in Miami with my mother and three of her friends. They were trying to hook me up with one of their sons. We ate breakfast at the *Holiday Inn* where we were staying. I'm sure they have video surveillance," July said.

Then, apparently July's appointment was done, as she stood up and walked haughtily out.

Netta groaned, because she was stuck there for at least another half hour while her technician murmured about how Netta should be charged with a crime for neglecting her nails so badly.

When Netta left the salon, she felt as though she had been released from prison. She headed back to the inn. She'd eaten breakfast a long time ago and her stomach was protesting loudly. She figured she would eat first, then call Danny and tell him what she learned.

The sandwiches were delicious, but Netta was in the mood for a snack. She saw a piece of cake with her name on it on the counter. She figured that Justine must have left it for her.

She would have to give Justine a raise, because not only did she practically run the inn on her own, she also took great care of Netta.

She had just about reached her mouth with a forkful of moist, chocolate cake when Justine ran up and slapped the fork out of her hand. It fell to the floor with a loud clatter.

Netta gave her best friend a startled look.

"What in the world is wrong with you?" she asked. "The cake had my name on it."

"I had a vision," Justine said, her voice shaking. "I saw you eating a bite of cake and falling to the floor dead."

TWENTY-THREE

Netta called Danny.

"I talked to July. She has an alibi that will likely check out. But I was wondering if you could come to the inn and bring an evidence bag."

Netta hated the shakiness in her voice.

Danny didn't ask questions and arrived within a couple of minutes. A uniformed officer arrived soon after. Netta pointed to the cake.

She couldn't very well tell him that Justine had seen a vision of the future.

"This was left for me. It had my name on it. Justine never saw who delivered it, which means that the person slipped in and out quickly. I hope that I'm wrong, but I think this qualifies as hinky."

"You were right to call. Considering two incidents already targeted you, this could be another attack. I'd rather be safe than sorry," he said. "Please bag this and take it to the forensic lab," he said to the uniform. "Ask them to test for ricin poisoning. And do not directly handle this cake under any circumstances."

"Yes sir," said the officer, looking a little bit frightened.

Danny turned to Netta and Justine.

"Did either of you touch it?"

They both shook their heads no, but hurried to scrub their hands anyway.

Danny pulled another pair of plastic gloves from his pants pocket. He scooped up the small bits of cake that had fallen to the floor with a plastic spoon and put them in a baggie that emerged from another pocket.

He grabbed paper towels and cleanser from the inn kitchen and scrubbed the floor. Then, he scrubbed it again.

He put the gloves and the paper towels in a plastic bag, and then into a paper evidence bag.

"I'll take this back to the lab. They know how to properly dispose of potentially harmful material. I'll let you know as soon as I get the results."

Netta nodded, her heart still racing. She felt so thankful she had Justine, or she would have turned into yet another dead body in the case.

And speaking of...

She wrote down the information she'd learned from July for Danny, her hand shaking so hard that she could barely read her writing. She wasn't sure if she was more angry or more scared, but she was determined that she would help solve this mystery.

"Are you going to be okay?" Danny asked softly.

Netta nodded and gritted her teeth.

"I'll be fine. I should have known not to eat something that appeared out of nowhere."

Danny thanked both women and left with his evidence. Two hours later, he called Netta. The cake had been laced with ricin powder – enough to have killed four adult men.

Someone had tried to kill Netta.

Now, she was angry. Whoever was behind this went too far. She fought to steady her voice.

"Thank you for letting me know. I'm going to go visit July's mother. I'll tell her I'm a liaison consulting for you. If she calls, you can have my back."

She hung up before Danny could protest.

Both Emily and Justine told her not to go.

"Someone is trying to kill you!" Justine said.

"And being a ghost can be fun, but I really miss being alive," Emily said. "I don't want you to be a ghost, too."

"If it was up to you two, you'd lock me in the closet until the case was over," Netta said.

Emily and Justine looked at each other as though that wasn't such a bad idea. Netta sighed, grabbed her keys, and headed out to visit July's mom.

A maid answered the door of the opulent house in the nicest neighborhood in Miami, then led Netta to a formal sitting room.

"Please wait here. Ms. Donovan will be with you shortly," she said in a snippy voice. Netta could tell that the maid had looked her over and found her lacking.

July's mom, June Donovan, was a character. She obviously thought that since she had a lot of money she was better than everyone.

"My daughter told me that you would be visiting me," she said in a condescending voice. "I will tell you that she was with us that morning when that dreadful man was killed."

June appraised Netta's appearance much like the maid had.

"You know, you might find someone to take care of you if you acted more like a lady than a fish."

Netta coughed to keep from laughing. She figured that

her hilarity would not be appreciated, as June appeared serious.

"That's July's problem, too. She's too picky. She wants the perfect, good-looking, rich man who will tolerate her wild ways. I invited her to come up here to meet the son of one of my friends. He would be a *good* husband for her," June said.

"I'm sure she'll settle down when she finds someone to love," Netta said, rising to her feet. She had to get out of here before she lost too many brain cells.

"Love is for poor people. People like us marry for social standing and class," June replied.

"Thank you for your time," Netta said, practically running out of the house and to her car. As she settled into the driver's seat, she reflected that although her visit had yielded no outright revelations, she had gained a better understanding of why July acted the way she did.

Netta felt sorry for her. If Netta's mother had acted that way, Netta would have likely been off her rocker, too.

Using her Bluetooth connection, she called Danny to tell him what she learned. As she recounted it, she had to admit it didn't amount to much.

When would they break this case?!

TWENTY-FOUR

When Netta got back to the inn, she felt restless, so she decided that she would go for a walk on the beach. She stared out into the ocean, watching the waves break against the sand.

She knew that she was missing something but wasn't sure what it was. This whole case had been a study in frustration. The women suspects had been eliminated. So, where did that leave the investigation?

She suddenly thought of one place that she hadn't visited in her quest for clues. Technically, she shouldn't go there, but if she didn't find anything useful, then no one would need to know about the trip.

If she *did* find something, then it would help close the case and Danny wouldn't be quite as mad at her. Or he would get over it.

It was easy to break into Kevin's house. The first thing she noticed was that it was a huge mess. She didn't know if the police had gone through the house and torn it up, or if someone else had been there looking for something.

She walked slowly around the living room, touching

bookshelves, a couch, tables. Then, when she touched one of the chairs, she saw a picture of a gold bar and caught her breath.

This was the second time she had seen a vision of a gold bar, and the second time that she hadn't been able to read the inscription on it. As before, the image had faded too quickly.

She saw dishes strewn around the room, as though someone had turned a table over in their eagerness to look beneath it. She saw a cup half-hidden under the couch. When she touched it, she had another vision.

The cup was filled with castor beans.

What might that mean?

The vision faded. Netta looked inside the cup, making sure that she used the bottom of her shirt to handle it. She discovered powder stuck to the bottom. She made a mental note to call Danny later so that he could have it tested.

She carefully stepped over the flotsam and jetsam and found Kevin's office. All of the drawers in the filing cabinet were open. Papers and folders lay everywhere. It looked like someone had just grabbed a handful and thrown them in the air, letting them fall where they may.

Bending down, she rifled through some of the papers for useful information and to see if they provoked further visions. She received two interesting images: castor beans again, and aerosol cans.

Maybe her visions centered on the way Kevin died, since the ricin gas that killed him had likely been administered by aerosol. But this second round of visions provoked a question. Was Netta seeing these images as reflections of Kevin's death, or had he created, sold, or transported chemical weapons?

Considering the fact that someone had already gone

through Kevin's office, she figured that anything deeply incriminating would have been removed already, so she headed into his bedroom.

She stood in the doorway and assessed the room. It had obviously been tossed like the rest of the apartment, but she had a feeling that there was something here.

Her gut instincts led her over to Kevin's bed. She felt a little creepy being near it, but there was something here. She could feel it.

She tentatively touched the mattress, and an image popped into her mind. There was a laptop sewn into the underside.

Hefting the mattress over, she pulled out the crude stitches and retrieved a battered silver laptop.

Oddly, the machine wasn't password locked but most of the files were encrypted. Since technical savvy wasn't one of her witchy powers, she clicked on his email account.

The last message was from Knoll: *You better watch your back. No one gets to leave the group without facing the consequences.*

That message raised the hairs on the back of her neck. Could Knoll have killed Kevin? That would certainly explain how Knoll managed to get over Kevin's death so quickly. What group were they a part of? Did this have anything to do with the murder of Marliss' father?

She wiped her prints off the machine, and quickly stuffed it back into the mattress. The last thing she needed was to become a suspect for Kevin's murder because her fingerprints were all over the evidence. Danny would know she didn't do it, but he didn't work in a vacuum.

Netta called Danny, who answered on the first ring.

"Before you yell at me, hear me out," Netta said.

Danny groaned loudly, but he didn't say anything.

"I checked out Kevin's house and found a couple of clues that you need to collect," Netta said. "First, there is a cup half hidden under the couch that contains a powdery residue. I suspect that if you were to run tests on it, you would find ricin."

"How did you find that?" Danny asked.

"A hunch," Netta said. Then before Danny could say anything else, she went on. "There is also a laptop in his mattress – on the underside of it. He had sewn it in there. There are a bunch of encrypted files on it and a very interesting email from Knoll warning Kevin to watch his back."

"How did you know to look there?" Danny asked.

"I thought about where I would hide something that had important information that other people might want to get their hands on," she answered.

"Are you still there?" he asked.

"Yes," she answered.

"We've talked about you breaking and entering. You can't do that. *It is against the law,*" Danny admonished. "Thank you for the clues, but you have got to stop breaking into places." He sighed heavily, knowing that he may as well be talking to himself.

"Get out of there, so I can send some people to collect what you found."

TWENTY-FIVE

anny was very pleased with the information that Netta had found, although he wasn't too happy with how she found it.

Actually, he wasn't *sure* how she found it. But he didn't press the issue.

The threatening email was a great clue, although if anyone discovered how he came by it, the information would never be allowed in court. But maybe he could use the information to get Knoll to confess to murdering Kevin, or to tell Danny what he knew about the crime.

Knoll answered his phone right away, and Danny asked him to come into the station to talk about the case.

"Did you find out who killed Kevin? That has me all torn up. He was my friend," Knoll said.

"I just really need you to come in. I don't want to discuss details over the phone," Danny said.

"Okay. I'll be there in half an hour," Knoll said.

When Knoll arrived, Danny led him to an interrogation room. He decided to start off strong to knock Knoll off kilter.

"I've had some very credible informants tell me that you

were threatening Kevin because he wouldn't give you any more money for drugs."

"Who are these informants?" Knoll asked. His eyes bulged, and he drummed his fingers on the table in a steady beat. A vein on the side of his neck was throbbing.

He was agitated. That was good. Agitated people tended to be more forthcoming with information.

Danny ignored his question.

"I was told that you were in over your head because you owed your dealers quite a bit and you were desperate. Your suppliers were starting to get antsy and had threatened to break some kneecaps, or worse, if you didn't pay up.

"Everyone knows that Kevin carried around huge amounts of cash. Did you kill him for his cash? He didn't have any on him when he was found. Was there an argument and you killed him in the heat of the moment?"

Knoll had a shocked look on his face and he started to stutter.

"I didn't kill Kevin. I didn't need money from him anymore. Kevin had a friend that he was working for—that's how he got enough money to help me out.

"Kevin got me a job, too. I'm clean. I haven't been taking drugs for at least a month now."

"Who is this friend?" Danny asked.

Knoll turned slightly pale and shook his head.

"Nuh-uh. No way I'm telling you that. He's way scarier than the police. No matter what y'all could do to me, he'd do a million times worse. Forget it." Knoll crossed his arms, leaned back in his chair, and pressed his lips tightly closed.

Danny wondered who in *Siren Key* could be that scary. It must be someone from out of town.

Then it was as though a lightbulb came on inside Knoll's head.

"I couldn't have killed Kevin. I was in jail."

Danny left the room to go check out Knoll's alibi. The man was telling the truth. He had landed in lockup because he had gotten into a fight with someone at a bar. They had been talking smack to each other. Knoll followed the guy out of the bar, grabbed a tire iron from his truck, and hit the guy over the head. Someone called the police and Knoll went to jail, charged with aggravated assault. He posted bond to walk free.

Frustrated, Danny went back into the interrogation room to tell Knoll he could go. With a smug look, Knoll strolled out like he had just won a major battle.

Heading back to his office, Danny called Netta.

"Hey, I just wanted to let you know that the cup you found did have ricin in it," Danny said. "This stuff is everywhere."

Netta considered.

"I don't think that Kevin and I are important enough to inspire a killer to make ricin just to use on us. There has to be a larger reason. Do you think that someone is planning an attack on the city? The *Reef Riot* kicks off tonight," Netta said.

The *Reef Riot* was a carnival event that happened every year, a fundraiser that supported coral reefs in the area. There were rides, singers, dancing, games, and more. It drew big, boisterous crowds.

"I don't know. That is certainly one idea. Most locals will be there tonight, plus a whole bunch of tourists. Any other thoughts on the situation?" Danny asked.

Although he hated to keep involving Netta, he couldn't deny that she had come up with more clues than he had.

Netta was quiet for a minute, thinking it through.

"I'll have to get back to you," she said.

"Do you want to go to the *Reef Riot* with me tonight?" Danny asked.

"I'll think about that, too, and get back to you," Netta answered.

After they hung up, Danny sat back in the chair. He had a feeling that everything was going to come to a head soon, and if he didn't figure out what was going on, there would be a lot more people hurt or killed.

His thoughts turned toward Netta again. He had no idea what made him ask her to go with him to tonight's carnival. He'd already made a pact with himself that he wouldn't attempt romance until the case was solved.

He could almost believe that the carnival was the next logical place to look for clues. And, because Netta had been a huge help, taking her to the event offered him a chance to thank her for her work.

He smiled at that thought.

Nice try, dude.

He might fool other people, but not himself.

TWENTY-SIX

Netta's mind raced in a million different directions. Although she knew that she should focus on the case, she couldn't help thinking about Danny's impromptu invitation.

Did he invite her to the *Reef Riot* because he thought that a criminal event was going to happen there? Or was he inviting her for more personal reasons?

She figured it was the first option. He had been friendly toward her but hadn't shown any romantic interest. He had kissed her cheek, sure. But she kissed her granny on the cheek, so that really didn't mean anything.

She just hoped that he hadn't put her in the same category as his granny.

Netta tried to tamp down all the feelings she had for the detective. She told herself that she was a grown woman, running two businesses, and had no time for 'little girl, fairy tale romances.'

But in her heart of hearts, she still wanted that fairy tale.

Closing her eyes, she told herself that there were more important things to think about than Danny. She had to figure out what was going on before more people, like herself, were hurt or killed. At this point, it seemed like it was only a matter of time before full-on chaos broke out.

Turning her attention toward the case, she thought about Knoll. He obviously didn't kill Kevin because he had the best alibi out of all of the suspects.

But she had a sneaking suspicion that he knew who murdered his friend but was too terrified to talk.

Who could this "Mr. Big" be?

Racking her brain, Netta tried to picture all of the people in town who could possibly have enough money and influence to get an "organization" started.

Kevin's father did. But even if father and son weren't getting along, would he really have his own son killed?

Another question was what kind of organization was Knoll referring to? The Mafia had long since fizzled out in the area. Many larger cities were plagued by gangs, but there wasn't any gang activity in *Siren Key*. At least, not the kind that would result in someone's death from a terroristic weapon.

There was always a possibility that a terrorist or two could lurk in the lovely little town. After all, the terrorists who orchestrated the September 11 attacks on the World Trade Centers in New York had to have stayed somewhere before executing their plan.

Netta picked up her phone and was about to call Drake to find out if he had discovered anything new. She really wanted to know about the metallic bits found on Kevin's face and neck. Drake said that they had been microscopic and he had almost missed them. But he'd taken swabs of them and sent them to the lab.

She put her phone back down again. Either Drake or

Danny would call her if the forensic lab came up with any new evidence.

Wouldn't they?

Netta paced back and forth across the inn lobby and snack area.

"Girl, you are going to wear a path in the floor if you don't stop," Emily said. "You're going to have to give extra diving lessons just to pay for a new floor."

"I can't help it. I know that I am missing something," Netta said. "It's frustrating me."

Justine, her eyes vacant, her face pale, pointed at Netta.

"Justine, what's wrong?" Netta asked urgently.

"There is a shadow. A black shadow. It's hovering over you. You're in grave danger. It's close," Justine said, in a low monotone voice. "It's following you. You can't hide from it."

Netta felt her heart drop. Justine's visions were always right. They might be vague and difficult to interpret until it was almost too late, but they were always spot on.

Walking over to Justine, Netta put her arm around her friend and gently shook her from her trance.

Justine's eyes cleared and she looked at Netta.

"Oh, my goodness. Someone is going to try to kill you again. You should lock yourself in your bedroom and not come out until this case is solved. I'll bring you food and water."

Netta laughed, softly.

"Honey, you know I can't do that. Besides, you told me yourself it wouldn't do any good. You said that I couldn't hide from the danger and that it would find me wherever I go. I have to figure out who is after me and stop them from getting to me."

"You have to be very careful," Justine begged. "I can't

lose you, too. You're like my sister, and you, Maven, Emily, and the kitties are the only family I have left."

Netta smiled reassuringly at her friend.

"I promise that I will be very careful. I know that we are getting close to solving this puzzle. Then, our world can return to normal."

"I hope so," Justine said.

After making herself a cup of hot orange spice tea, Netta sat down at one of the tables. There was a tickle in the back of her mind that was bothering her. She thought back to all the people she'd talked to since Kevin was killed.

Suddenly a light bulb came on.

She remembered two conversations she had overheard and everything made sense.

Her heart racing, she picked up her phone. She tried to dial Danny's number, but her fingers were shaking too hard.

She was just about to press the last digit when she gave a little squeal. Her phone rang. It was one of the people she had desperately been wanting to talk to.

"Hi, Netta, how are you doing?" Drake asked.

"Great, you?" Netta asked, chomping at the bit to get the niceties over with. She needed to hear news that would confirm her suspicions.

"I got the test results back from the lab," Drake said.

TWENTY-SEVEN

Netta's heart was racing. This was the clue she had been waiting for. If Drake said what she thought he'd say, then she'd know the killer's identity.

"I'm having trouble getting hold of Danny. I knew the two of you were unofficially working together on this case, so I thought I would give you a call," Drake said.

"I appreciate that," Netta said. "What did you learn?"

"Well, as you know, the lab found metallic trace evidence on Kevin's face and neck. I wasn't sure what it was, so I had it tested," Drake said.

Please get to the point.

"What did the lab find?"

"They were gold f—" Suddenly his words broke off.

Netta heard two loud thumps.

"Drake. Drake, are you there? Are you okay?" Netta frantically asked. A sinking feeling had developed in her gut and she thought that she was going to be sick.

"Sorry, Netta. Drake can't talk right now," a muffled voice came over the phone. "He has a bit of a headache and is all tied up."

The person laughed as though their joke was funny and original. Netta thought that it was neither.

"Sargasso, can you pop over to the medical examiner's office and see what is going on for me?" Netta asked, grateful once again for her familiar's skills in teleportation.

"Sure. Caspia, stay here. I'll be right back," Sargasso answered, and instantly disappeared.

He was gone for what seemed like forever, although in reality it was only a couple of minutes.

Even though she expected him, Netta started when Sargasso apparated back into the room. He had a worried look on his face. The area between his ears furrowed like an anxious old man's.

"What did you see?" Netta anxiously asked.

"It doesn't look good," Sargasso answered. "His phone is off the hook. There is blood splatter on his desk and the floor. A brick is lying off to the side, like someone had tossed it away. It had hair and blood on it. There were black scuff marks on the floor like someone had been dragged away."

Sargasso pumped up his chest.

"Someone whacked the doc and dragged him off," he pronounced dramatically.

"Anything else?" Netta asked, a little breathlessly.

"Papers were thrown everywhere. The file with Kevin's name on it still sat on Drake's desk, but it was empty. Whoever attacked the doctor took all his notes about the murder."

Then Sargasso peered at Netta.

"The person also left a note for you."

Sargasso took out a piece of paper that he had tucked under his tiny front leg. In printed block handwriting, the note read: *We'll be seeing you soon, Netta.*

There was no overt threat on the paper but the message

was clear. Whoever had killed Kevin and hauled Drake away planned to come after her.

Netta took a deep breath to try to calm herself. She must not panic. Panicking would only make her unable to think properly. Her mind worked furiously.

What could Drake have known that would make him such an immediate threat?

What was he about to say when the attacker struck?

Justine's voice broke into her thoughts.

"If they kidnapped him, he's probably still alive. If they'd killed him, they would have left the body behind because dead men don't talk.

"They probably took Drake to find out what he knows and with whom he's shared the knowledge," Justine reasoned. "That means that there is still plenty of time to find him, because I know Drake and he won't talk."

Netta nodded. Justine made a lot of sense.

Unfortunately, Drake's stubbornness cut both ways: once the bad guys figured out that he wouldn't talk, they'd kill him just to eliminate loose ends.

The other issue that needed immediate attention was that Netta was now in extreme danger. Whoever had whacked and taken Drake knew that he had been on the phone with her. Who knows how much of their conversation the assailant had actually overheard.

In sum: if the assailant thought Netta knew 'too much', she was in as much danger as Drake had been.

Grabbing her phone, she called Danny, but just as Drake had said, he wasn't answering his phone.

Where in the world could he be when I need him most?

Netta only prayed that the bad guys hadn't attacked him, too.

When she reached Danny's voice mail, she said, "Drake

called to give me some information, but before he could get to it, someone hit him in the head with a brick and kidnapped him. I think that they are going to kill him.

"Call me as soon as you get this message."

She mentally reviewed the assailant's taunting words: "Sorry, Netta. Drake can't talk right now. He has a bit of a headache and is all tied up."

The person on the phone had tried to disguise his voice, but there was something oddly familiar about it.

Suddenly the puzzle pieces fell into place. She got it.

She called Danny back, and despite her intense excitement, tried to talk slowly and clearly.

"Danny, I know who killed Kevin and who is about to kill Drake." She told him where to meet her and then started out the door.

Justine wrung her hands.

"Please be extra, extra careful. The black shadow that represents death has now attached itself to your back. You are in so much danger, Netta! I know it's useless to ask that you wait for Danny..." Despite her words, Justine's eyes implored Netta to stay.

Netta hugged her hard.

"I promise I will be very careful and I will return in one piece. Hold down the fort."

Justine nodded, but Netta could see the fear that clouded her friend's face. She, too, felt a wave of anxiety, but there was no time to wait for Danny.

Her friend was in danger, and she had to save him.

TWENTY-EIGHT

Danny and Netta showed up at the same time. The booth they sought was off to one side of the carnival. Victor had a refrigerator truck in which he kept his stock, so he needed a huge space.

As they approached, they saw Victor hurrying about, loading supplies into the truck. The two detectives parted, and Netta walked forward alone.

When Netta drew within a few feet of Victor, he smiled at her and pulled out a huge knife.

"I was hoping to see you before I left. You are way too nosy for your own good," he said. "I'm going to cut you up into pretty little ribbons and feed your body parts to the fish. You can be a part of the ocean that you love so well. Aren't I a sweetheart for always thinking of others?"

Victor didn't see Danny approaching from behind, so Netta decided to keep him talking.

"You had it made with your restaurants. You would have been a millionaire several times over if you had stuck with your desserts and Italian food," Netta told him.

"I found a way to make those millions a lot faster,"

Victor said, shrugging. "A man like me isn't supposed to slave away in the kitchen when there are other, more interesting, things that I could be doing."

"Like killing people?" Netta asked.

"If necessary," Victor shrugged.

Danny lunged into sight and grabbed Victor's knife arm. Victor twisted away and swiped at Danny's face. The detective had brought a gun to a knife fight, though.

He pulled his service pistol from his holster.

"Drop it," Danny ordered.

Victor hesitated, torn among a series of conflicting impulses, but then decided that dropping the knife was his best option.

"Where is Drake?" Netta asked. "What did you do to him?"

Victor shrugged and smiled.

"He's just chilling right now. What can I say?"

Just then, Netta heard some faint banging that was coming from the refrigerator truck. She looked at Victor. A dark look had come over his face.

She ran over to the truck and threw open the doors. Drake sat among several cakes and other delicacies, tied up and shivering. The temperature had been turned down to twenty degrees.

Victor had turned the refrigerator truck into a freezer truck.

Netta pulled the gag off of Drake.

"It's about time you got here. I thought I was going to have to rescue myself."

"It's not as much fun that way," Netta said. "And isn't it the man who's supposed to be rescuing the damsel in distress?"

"You've read too many fairy tales that were written a

long t-t-time ago. In today's world, women can be the knights in shining armor if they want to b-b-be," Drake stammered, his teeth chattering as Netta removed the around his ankles.

"Does that make you the dude in distress?" Netta said, helping Drake to his feet.

He smiled as his shivers grew into outright tremors.

"It does, and this dude appreciates the r-r-rescue."

Netta and Drake walked carefully out of the truck just as cops and homeland security agents swarmed the area. The agents took custody of Victor.

Danny walked over to Drake and his heroine. Netta fought to untie the tight knots around Drake's wrists. Danny pulled a knife out of his pocket and started to saw through the ropes.

"That's too easy," Netta said.

Drake laughed softly.

"Right now, I'm good with easy," he said, rubbing the circulation back into his chafed wrists and hands. "I was afraid that I was going to have to chew my way through a gag, and then two sets of rope."

"Nah," Netta said. "We wouldn't have left you hanging. We just had to deal with Victor first."

Victor sat on the ground. Two cops stood by with their guns trained on him. Danny asked them to put out an All Points Bulletin on Knoll Curry, as he now believed that after Victor had killed Kevin, he'd replaced him with Knoll as his right-hand-man.

"Kevin was talking too much, getting way too cocky," Victor growled. "I was afraid that either he'd get us all caught, or he'd try something crazy like taking over the organization.

"Apparently he didn't like me telling him to shut it, and

said he'd rather just walk away from the business."

Victor gave a nasty smile.

"He wanted to leave," the killer shrugged. "So I helped him leave."

With that admission, the homeland security agents exchanged a glance.

"Right. We'll take it from here," the taller one said. The two cops guarding Victor hauled him to his feet and handed him over to the feds. They stood there holding him by the upper arms and watched the other police personnel search his refrigerator truck.

They sliced open all of the food packets in the truck, dissecting everything from fancy cakes to 5-layer lasagnas. Inside each food item, they found a bottle jar, plastic baggie full of powder, or a small aerosol can.

It appears that Victor had decided that chemical weapons were easy to make, and with all of the unrest in the world, he could amass plenty of buyers.

At first, he shipped everything at night, an operation that Netta unknowingly witnessed that night on the beach by her inn.

However, Victor had an important buyer who wanted more product immediately. So, instead of using another boat, Victor concealed the weapons in his cakes and pasta dishes, intending to drive them to a large port nearby, where his client's ship was waiting.

"Ricin was the easiest and cheapest weapon to make. And profitable? Come on! I could bring in a hundred times the manufacturing cost without even pushing myself," Victor boasted.

"It *murders* people," Netta said. "Your concoctions kill at least as many people as street drugs kill. But the difference is that ricin slaughters *innocents*, Victor. Folks who aren't knowingly taking any risks, who just happen to be in the wrong place at the wrong time."

"Not my problem," Victor shrugged. "It's the price of war."

TWENTY-NINE

"How did you figure everything out?"

Danny looked at Netta, eyes shining with pride and wonder.

She liked that.

Everyone—Homeland Security, cops, even Victor himself—leaned in to listen. Netta cleared her throat and dove in.

"My first clue was when I overheard the conversation between Victor and Knoll about deliveries. It caught my ear because up until that time, Victor's restaurant had never delivered anything. In fact, people used to complain about that!"

Victor grunted and rolled his eyes, but said nothing.

"Then, I heard Knoll and Scylla talking about Kevin being involved with a drug syndicate. I thought that Knoll's claims could be legit since he implicated himself in the whole mess when he admitted to breaking into Kevin's house.

"Also, there were the regular, large deposits into Kevin's bank accounts. Everyone knew his father wasn't giving him a dime, so the money had to come from somewhere. And there aren't too many jobs that pay cash, especially not for large sums."

Everyone nodded. So far, everything she said made perfect sense.

"And one night, I woke up and watched folks load boxes from the beach near the inn onto a boat. Soon after, the Coast Guard finds a pair of bodies, dead from ricin poisoning, at the scene of a boating accident.

"That was the same poison that killed Kevin, so there had to be a link. Not too many people are killed that way."

She looked around to make sure everyone was following her logic.

"And that's not all."

One of the Homeland Security agents chuckled and shook her head, then nodded for Netta to go on.

"Someone tried to kill me with a piece of cake laced with ricin. Not a common poison but here it was again, and this time it was in chocolate cake, which everyone knows I wouldn't be able to resist. After I broke into Kevin's house—"

That raised a few eyebrows among the listening cops.

"I found a cup with ricin in it, which I think indicates that Kevin was probably poisoned two ways to make sure that he was good and dead.

"Kevin's laptop held the threat from Knoll warning him about leaving the organization, and I didn't think that it would be the bowling league or the boy scouts. The warning made even more sense when Knoll claimed that he worked for someone who was very scary – even scarier than the police."

At that, Victor smiled, seemingly proud of his perceived badness. Danny rolled his eyes.

"The last clue was that Drake managed to say, 'Gold f —", before he was hit on the head and kidnapped. I think he was trying to say 'gold flakes', maybe the kind used to decorate fancy desserts. That led me straight to Victor."

Drake nodded, and Netta spread her hands wide like a magician after a successful trick.

"Ta-dah! I knew Victor would be here, so I called Danny and asked him to meet me."

Netta couldn't tell them about her magical visions of gold bars because no one in the audience knew that she was a witch. That would remain her little secret.

"I would have gotten away with everything if you hadn't stuck your nose into my business," Victor said. "I tried to frighten you away, but you wouldn't scare," he told Netta.

"All you did was make me angry and more determined to figure out who was hurting my town," Netta said evenly.

"Take him away," Danny said to the feds, who lost no time in hustling Victor toward their big, dark SUVs. As the killer stumbled along, he shouted over his shoulder that the baked goods in his refrigerator truck cost a fortune to make.

"I expect to be reimbursed for those!" he yelped. "Every last cake! Do you hear me, Sussex?"

"The cakes are evidence," Danny called. "And you are officially out of business – both your restaurants and your chemical weapons. You don't have anything to worry about except making sure that you get the numbers right on all of those license plates you will be making in prison."

Once Victor was gone. Drake started making his own fuss.

"I'm fine. I'm a doctor and I would know if I needed to go to the doctor," he said loudly.

"Sir, you need to get your heiney on this gurney or I'll

do it for you," said the woman EMT, Tamika Kent, who looked strong enough to do exactly that.

"I'm fine. I was just a little chilled for a bit," Drake said.

"You were hit on the head and put on ice," Danny said.

"A concussion and hypothermia are nothing to mess around with," said Tamika. "You need to let us check you out at the hospital."

"I tell you that I'm a doctor, and I'm fine," Drake said.

"He's been whacked in the head and doesn't know what he's talking about," Danny said and turned to his friend. "Your professional opinion is invalid and overruled. Get on that gurney, or I will tase you so that you won't be able to decide for yourself."

Drake heaved a huge sigh as though he were being badly used.

"I'm outnumbered. I'll go, but I'm not going to like it," he said.

"You don't have to like it," Tamika said, advancing on Drake. He climbed carefully up onto the gurney and laid down.

"I might as well get a nap in," Drake said as he yawned loudly. "I am a little sleepy." Tamika rolled her eyes and she and her partner loaded Drake into their ambulance and drove off.

Netta laughed.

"If Justine wasn't sweet on Drake, I think that Tamika would make a perfect match for him. She would certainly be able to keep him in line."

Danny nodded.

"Now that the case is over, what do you say about having just a wee bit of fun? Will you go to the carnival with me?" he asked.

"I think that's a great idea," she said. "Are you buying dinner, too?"

"It's the least I can do, since I'm such a gentleman."

"Gentleman? Is that what you are? Let's get real—I helped solve your case so you owe me."

"So I do," Danny said, and laughed aloud.

THIRTY

Netta would never have guessed that she could have so much fun. Danny had a very sarcastic sense of humor, which matched hers perfectly. He was one of the few people who actually understood her smart-alecky humor.

They went on several rides together, and Netta teased that she whooped him at Bumper Cars and Go Karts.

The pair sat at the top of the Ferris Wheel when Netta's phone rang. It was from a private number.

"Hi, Netta Carlisle?" a familiar voice asked.

"Yes," she said hesitantly and cautiously.

"This is Paul King. I'm the documentary director who stayed at your inn and went on a dive with you."

"Yes, great to hear from you," Netta said, her heart beating a hard rhythm in her chest. She grabbed Danny's arm and squeezed it tightly. Did she dare hope?

"As you know, we canvassed the entire United States to find the five best scuba diving instructors in the country," Paul said.

"Yes, sir," said Netta, wishing that the director would get on with what he had to say.

"My D.P., Keith Parr, and I had an amazing time and thought that your presentation and your lessons were superb," Paul went on.

"Thank you," Netta said, her heart sinking. She could sense a "but" coming in.

"So, we decided that we would like to offer you the opportunity to be featured in our presentation," he said.

"Yes!" Netta almost screamed. Then, more calmly she said, "That would be an honor. I'm so excited."

"Terrific," Paul said. "Our assistant will be in touch with you to arrange all the fine details."

"That sounds great," Netta said. "I'm looking forward to it."

"I was also wondering if you could give me the information as to where you purchased those delicious cakes and desserts. I would love to give them as gifts to my friends and family," Paul said.

"I'm sorry to tell you that as of today, the man who made those cakes has officially gone out of business," Netta said.

"That's too bad," Paul said. "Those were amazing. But anyway, Keith and I are looking forward to seeing you soon."

When Netta got off the phone she was so excited that she was making the car wiggle all over the place. Danny clutched the sides.

"Be still!" he said. "You're going to tip us over."

"I can't help it," Netta said. "They chose me to be featured in their documentary. That is so amazing."

"I'm happy for you. But let's live through this ride and then we can celebrate," Danny said.

The ride was over quickly, and Netta felt beside herself with joy. This would mean a lot to the town. The documentaries usually focused on more than a single person or event. Perhaps the director would showcase the town, the shops, the locals. That could help repair the devastation that Victor had caused.

Netta felt suddenly hungry, so they headed over to the Philly Steak Sandwiches booth. They had just finished their enormous cheesesteaks when her phone rang again. Justine was with Drake at the hospital.

"The doctors determined that he had a mild concussion and they want to keep him here overnight for observation. But there's no frostbite, thanks to you. He'll be okay," Justine said. "I'm going to hang out here with him."

"That sounds great," Netta said. Then she told Justine about the documentary.

"Whoo-hoo!" Justine yelled. Netta laughed when she heard a nurse shush her.

Danny and Netta stayed until the carnival closed, eating cotton candy and funnel cake. By midnight, Netta was pretty sure her belly was going to explode.

Danny followed her to the inn and walked her to the door.

He opened his mouth to say something but Netta put her finger on Danny's lips and shook her head.

"We'll take everything slow and see where it goes. It's been a long time since we've been together socially, and we need to get to know each other again."

Danny nodded, although he looked a little disappointed. Then, he smiled, hugged her, and dropped a kiss on her cheek. He waited until he knew she was safely inside and left.

With a huge smile on her flushed face, she went upstairs to her bedroom where Emily, Sargasso, and Caspia waited for her.

"How did it go?" Emily asked eagerly, as a greeting.

"Let's say *very* well," Netta told her.

She headed into the bathroom and started brushing her teeth. Emily and the kittens followed her.

"Did he kiss you?" Emily asked.

Netta just smiled at her and pointed to the toothbrush in her mouth.

Sargasso spoke up.

"That means that she didn't even get a goodnight kiss. He just won her some cheap stuffed animal at one of the booths. Since he's a cop, it was probably one of the shooting booths."

"It was at the baseball throwing game, I'll have you know," Netta said, when she was finished. She darted back into the bedroom and threw the aforementioned stuffed animal at the kitties as Emily disappeared with a giggle.

Netta snuggled into bed and thought about the day.

She had solved the case, saved her friend, and had a first date with the man she had been in love with since she was a teenager.

But she wanted to make sure that she was in love with the man and not someone that she invented in her mind with Danny's face.

They could take it slow. They had all the time in the world to get to know each other.

With that thought, she fell into a deep sleep with a huge smile on her face.

· · ·

TO BE CONTINUED...

To get a sneak peek about Danny and Netta's next encounter click here to join my newsletter: https://www.subscribepage.com/corrinewinters

PREVIEW

Hey Readers!

Check out a preview of another book from Corrine Winters!

Dramatic Paws

By Corrine Winters

THIRTY-ONE

After 9:00 every night, the Broken Broom Pub became the hippest place in the little town of Cauchemar, Louisiana.

During the day, the Broken Broom was a glorified cafe, serving food and drinks to people of all ages, just the same as any other restaurant in town. They even kept a high-chair around and offered chicken nuggets and quesadillas for picky, sticky-handed children. They served syrupy lattes to teenagers who wanted to feel sophisticated but didn't actually like the taste of coffee.

But as soon as 9:00 hit, the proprietress, Ember McNair, turned out everyone under the age of twenty-one, and the Broken Broom magically transformed into Cauchemar's one and only option for anything like nightlife.

Of course, this business model kept Ember busy with her pub night and day. Luckily, busy was how Ember liked it.

It's busy enough tonight, all right, Ember thought as she made her way through the full tables, careful not to bump anyone with her hips. On nights like this, Ember wished she could afford to pay a bouncer.

She reached the bar and rapped at it to get the attention of Lyndsy, her bartender. Lyndsy looked up sharply from where she'd been chatting with one of the waitresses.

"Gin and tonic," Ember said. "Table seven's been waiting on it a while. They just grabbed me to send back a reminder."

"Oh, shoot, sorry, I thought I sent that out," Lyndsy said. She was usually on-the-ball, but tonight she looked distracted.

Ember turned to the waitress, Tara. She looked sour-faced, too.

"Everything all right?" Ember asked.

"It's fine," Lyndsy said, too quickly, already pouring out the shot of gin. "Nothing to worry about."

Tara shot Lyndsy a sideways look and scoffed. "*Yes, worry.* Laura Hall and her hideous cronies are here."

Ember watched Lyndsy, concerned. She knew Lyndsy had some bad history with those women. Lyndsy looked hyperfocused on not overfilling the tonic in the drink she was making, like she was worried she might spill. When Ember looked closer, she saw that Lyndsy's hands were shaking.

Meanwhile, Tara kept talking. "I can*not* serve them, you understand me? I refuse. You should have heard them just now. 'We want the *fanciest* wine you've got. None of that swill you normally serve.' Like, if you hate it so much, go someplace else?"

"All right," Ember said. "Tara, you take that G&T over to seven. I'll get Laura and the others."

Ember didn't mind throwing herself into the line of fire. She had a tough hide.

"What's the best wine we've got tonight?" Ember asks Lyndsy. Being a good bartender, Lyndsy also acted as something of an unofficial sommelier for the Broken Broom.

Lyndsy didn't answer, just plucked up a nearby bottle, uncorked it, and started pouring. Ember didn't want to push her on it, so she grabbed a nearby tray and loaded the three glasses onto it before leaving the bar and going off to find Laura Hall and her crew.

Jake Peterson, still dressed in his slightly-crumpled suit from his long day of work, bumped against Ember as he fought his way toward the bar, nearly upending the glasses of wine. She had to whisper the quickest spell to keep them from tipping over and spilling.

"Watch where you're going," Jake growled, irritated.

Ember suppressed an eye-roll and moved on.

"Ember," Laura practically shouted as Ember approached their table. "We were just talking about you!"

The other two women, Jayla Graham and Sheila Myers, giggled.

"I'll bet you were," Ember said, trying a pleasant smile.

"Great crowd tonight," Laura continued as Ember set the three wine glasses in front of them. "Lots of men in here. Friends of yours, are they?"

Another giggle from the peanut gallery.

"You must have really pleased a *lot* of guys to be so *very* popular," Laura continued, putting on a fake, saccharine smile. "Tell us, Em. How many of these men have you slept with this week?"

Ember couldn't help but laugh. Laura was known for trying to start rumors. Had ruined more than a couple people's lives and sanity that way. This wasn't the first time she'd gone after Ember, either, but Ember had learned that the quickest way to disarm the rumor was simply to roll her eyes at it and walk away. It told whoever was listening that she didn't care one way or another what was said about her, and best of all it tended to get Laura flaming mad.

So that's exactly what Ember did.

LUCKILY, Laura and the others only stuck around long enough to have a couple glasses.

"Glad to see the back of those witches," Lyndsy said darkly.

Ember bit back her instinctive defensive response to the term. Lyndsy didn't know that Ember was a witch, and they were both better off that way.

"Show me that bottle again that you served to them?"

Lyndsy handed it over. Ember turned it in her palm, investigating the label.

"Hmm, I haven't seen this one before. Did it come in with the latest shipment?"

"Couldn't tell ya," Lyndsy said. "I mean, we could check the inventory report."

Ember hesitated, considering, and then shrugged. "It's too late now, but in the future, if you don't recognize a label, let me know before we serve it. Prissy Laura Hall demands or no."

Lyndsy nodded. "Sorry about that. I will."

LATER, after the bar had cleared out and Ember had sent Lyndsy and the waitresses home to clean up on her own, the door suddenly blew open as if of its own accord.

At first, it looked like it might have been the wind that

caught it. But then a small, fluffy kitten came zipping through the open doorway and into the bar.

"Kali," Ember said, grateful to see her familiar. "You should have waited at home. I'll be finished soon."

Then, she noticed that her familiar had an agitated energy in her step, and had begun to pace restlessly.

Something was wrong.

"What is it?"

Kali spoke in a purring voice, which was uncharacteristically urgent and on-edge. "Laura Hall's car crashed into a tree on the way home from the Broken Broom tonight."

Ember gasped. She hadn't thought that Laura was that inebriated after just two glasses of wine. She wouldn't have let her drive home if she'd known.

"That's awful," she said. "Is Laura okay?"

Kali's whiskers twitched. "She's dead. And so are Jayla Graham and Sheila Myers. They were in the car."

"Oh my god. Did the crash kill them?"

"It isn't clear. The medical examiner has taken them for an autopsy."

A sudden, unseasonable chill blew in through the open door. In a little town like Cauchemar, this crash would mean a whole lot of trouble. A sinking feeling in her stomach, Ember walked across the room closed the door, double-locking it just for good measure.

THIRTY-TWO

The next morning, Ember woke up already feeling exhausted. She'd spent most of the night dreaming, something she did often. Occasionally, her dreams showed her snatches of the past or future, of other people's perspectives and emotions. She couldn't control when and how it happened, and she couldn't always identify what event or person she was being shown.

She also couldn't always tell what was a vision and what was just a normal, run-of-the-mill dream.

In her dream last night, someone had been angry. Very angry. She'd experienced the anger herself, the hatred coursing through her, making her shake and wringing her out like she had been dropped into an agitated washing machine.

She woke up bone-tired, still feeling the vestigial emotion the dream-world had thrust upon her.

Luckily, a quick glance in the mirror after her morning shower told her she didn't look as bad as she felt. Her long black hair hung in faint natural waves all the way down to her waist. There were no bags under her eyes, the color of which was, at present, a neutral cobalt.

Ember's eyes had a tendency to darken and lighten in hue according to her moods. "Like a mood ring," Ember's best friend, Sage, had once helpfully described it. This particular color meant she wasn't either happy or upset.

Just tired.

"You stay home," Ember advised Kali once she was dressed and heading out the door. "I have a feeling today is going to be murder."

Kali, curled up on the sofa, lifted her head and let out a sleepy, acquiescent yawn.

SHE HADN'T EVEN OPENED the restaurant yet when Sheriff Cedric Jamison rapped at the door.

"Morning," he said, more terse than she was used to seeing him. He was always a straightforward, no-nonsense kind of guy, but today he had an anxious energy about him that set Ember ill at ease. "Mind if I come in? Ask you a few questions?"

"Sure," she said, stepping back to let him in. She might not be feeling great, but she could only imagine how Cedric must be feeling, with three sudden deaths to get to the bottom of. "Make yourself comfortable."

Ember knew Cedric pretty well, had known him since they were kids. He'd been in the year above her during their school days, and he, like Ember, was part of the supernatural community in Cauchemar. Unlike Ember, however, Cedric was not a witch but rather a wolf shifter. Ember thought his wolf instincts and senses were probably a major help to him when it came to maintaining the law and sniffing out the various mysteries that cropped up around town.

Hopefully they would help him get to the bottom of this case, sooner rather than later.

As if he'd read Ember's mind, Cedric said, "So I'm sure you've heard about what happened to Laura Hall and her friends last night?"

"Yeah," Ember said, following Cedric up to the bar and rounding it as he sat down on one of the tall stools. She imagined he had probably been on his feet all night and was grateful for the chance to take a seat. She went ahead and poured him a cup of coffee, slid it across to the bar to him black, just like he liked it. "I was sorry to hear it."

He cut her a disbelieving look but didn't call her on it. "Thanks," he said, tilting the cup in her direction and then taking a cautious, grateful sip. She thought she saw some of the tension in him relax.

Ember smiled softly to herself. She was good at reading people, figuring out what they needed, a strength that was half magic and half just plain intuition. She liked to use this quality about herself to try to make people feel better, to help them when they were hurting.

"Well, I traced them back here," Cedric said. "Seems they were driving home after having a few."

"Just two glasses of wine apiece," Ember answered, addressing the unasked question. "They should have been fine to drive. You know I don't hesitate to take keys and call a cab if anyone looks like trouble." Even now, there were several sets of keys from last night locked up in the drawer under the cash register, waiting to be reclaimed by their hungover owners.

Cedric inclined his head. "Sure, sure," he said distract-edly, then flashed her a *wait a second* gesture. At first, she didn't know what it meant, but he swiveled the bar stool away and withdrew his vibrating phone from his pocket. Pressed a button to answer. "What's up?" he greeted whoever was on the other end of the line.

She did her best to keep busy as he spoke, but she couldn't help noticing his body language. His broad shoulders were hunching in increased tension, and he kept running his fingers anxiously through his shoulder-length blond hair.

"All right," he said tersely after a few minutes of listening. "I'm there right now. I'll ask. Yeah. Yeah. Okay, bye."

He hung up and turned back around.

"Ask me what?" Ember said, deciding not to try to pretend she wasn't eavesdropping on his end of the conversation.

"Jake Peterson," Cedric prompted.

After a pause, Ember nodded. "He was here last night, too. He comes in all the time. Glass of wine alone at the bar, makes a general nuisance of himself to my staff, heads home." Cedric was frowning, so Ember asked, "Why? Did he have something to do with the accident? I thought they crashed into a tree."

Cedric shook his head. "He's been found dead at his house. Cause unknown."

This was all getting to be very strange. Ember didn't know what to say.

"Four people dead after spending time at your bar?" Cedric asked, sounding the perfect mix between paternally concerned and accusing. "Doesn't exactly look good for you."

Ember scoffed, feeling a sudden surge of anger. "This is stupid. What are you saying--that I had something to do with this? Sure, I'm going to sabotage my own business by intentionally endangering my customers! You know me better than that, Cedric."

He rose from the bar and stepped away, coffee still only half-drained. "I'm not saying anything like that," he told her, voice taut. "I just hope you'll continue to cooperate as we figure out what happened last night."

Frowning, feeling angry and chastised, Ember took a few deep breaths before forcing herself to nod.

Cedric, evidently satisfied by this, tipped a nod at her, flipped a five dollar bill onto the bar to cover the coffee, and left.

THIRTY-THREE

When Cedric left, Ember felt agitated, so she decided to clean the front windows. It was a uniquely onerous task that she only tackled when she was already in a bad mood. That way, it wouldn't mess up a perfectly good day.

There was also something mildly therapeutic about applying a little elbow grease to the more stubborn spots.

For that reason, she saw Sage coming up to the Broken Broom from a block away. The shifter was in her human form, rather than her bat one, which was how she preferred to travel before sundown. "It's a lot slower," Sage often said, "but people are bound to take note of a bat during daytime."

Sage breezed into the pub and found Ember at the window.

"Washing the windows, huh?" She clicked her tongue sympathetically. Then, when Ember looked at her, and she took note of the deep-indigo hue of Ember's eyes--a color that always indicated a stormy mood--Sage let out a low whistle. "That bad?"

"Please tell me you're bringing good news," Ember answered with a groan.

The women dropped into chairs at a two-seater nearby.

"Actually, I'm looking for news," said Sage. "I figured you might know more than I do about what happened to those women. There's all sorts of talk...."

Of course there's talk, Ember thought, irritated. *This town loves to talk.*

She could only worry what they were talking about. How much talking they were doing about the Broken Broom.

Or about Ember herself.

"Yeah, I know enough," Ember admitted. "They were all at my pub. Laura and the others, *and* Jake."

Sage gasped, hand to her heart. "Not Jake Peterson?"

Ember nodded grimly. "I guess they found him dead. I don't know." She passed a hand over her face, feeling exhausted even though her day hadn't even properly begun. How was she going to make it all the way to tonight?

"I heard Laura was trying to start a fight in here last night," Sage said gently. When Ember looked at her, Sage was wearing her patented patient-listener expression, like an indulgent kindergarten teacher.

Sage had a calming, caring energy that always made Ember feel better. It was one of the things that made her such an amazing friend.

"Sure. You know how she was. Saying all sorts of nonsense." The specifics didn't seem worth repeating, and Sage didn't press her on it, so she gratefully left it at that. "I think she had some rumor she was trying to push about me. She was saying it all loud like she was hoping the whole world would pick it up."

"That sounds like her," Sage agreed, shaking her head

in disapproval. "Always finding trouble, and stirring it up for herself whenever she couldn't find it."

"But it's not like I did anything about it. I never let people like that bother me." Ember waved her hand vaguely, a gesture intended to communicate *I have more important things to worry about* by probably came off closer to *I'm feeling lost and overwhelmed.* "I served her, and that was that. Didn't even try to rush them out the door, either. When those ones get drinking, the tab usually goes pretty high."

"And who was Laura with again? I heard that there were three women, but nobody I talked to knew exactly who."

Ember couldn't help but wonder who Sage had been talking to. How did half the town already seem to know about this?

"Jayla Graham and Sheila Myers," Ember said.

"Ah yes. Her two shadows."

It was true. They'd all been part of this tight, mean-girl enclave as long as Ember had known them. Of course, it was always a pity when someone died so young and suddenly, but Ember doubted that the loss of those three in particular would really detract from the net happiness of this particular little community.

Jake, too. Ember had never had any problems with him personally, but she'd heard he was tough to get along with at work.

If, indeed, there was any connection between the deaths at all.

"They all connect back here," Ember sighed. "This is going to be terrible for business. You know how everyone in this town talks. I'll be the pub owner that murdered four people. Malice or negligence, even coincidence... nobody'll want to touch me with a thirty-foot pole."

"I'll eat here," Sage said kindly. "And I'll bring all my friends, too."

Ember smiled. "So... me?"

Sage scoffed, but she was laughing. "I have other friends. Or I'll make other friends, just so I can convince them that the Broken Broom is the best place in town and they have to spend all their money here." She squeezed Ember's hands again. "Don't worry. This'll blow over soon. You don't have anything to do with the murders, and Cedric is good at his job. He'll clear up the official record soon."

Ember was grateful to hear her friend say these words, even if she couldn't quite bring herself to believe them. She looked up at Sage with a hesitant smile and asked, "You don't think I had anything to do with it, do you?"

"Of course not," Sage said, and she took Ember's hand and squeezed it. "I know you wouldn't ever do anything like this. And I'll tell anyone the same, if they ask."

"Thank you." Ember was feeling a little misty-eyed. It was good to know she had a friend who stood by her side no matter what.

"Oh, look." Sage pointed through the freshly cleaned windows at where a small group of people was approaching the pub door. "Customers!"

"I guess some people don't read the papers," Ember said wryly, but she stood up anyway and gathered her cleaning supplies.

"I'll let you get to it," Sage said, swooping in to hug Ember tightly before breezing out the door as the customers were coming in.

Sage's words managed to sustain Ember throughout the

entire evening, which turned out to be much busier than Ember was anticipating. Perhaps word really hadn't gotten around yet, since the turnout was on par with a normal night.

Or else people were showing up tonight out of prurient interest.

Either way, Ember knew that these murders had to be solved as soon as possible. Or else she wasn't sure how long the Broken Broom--or its owner--would manage.

THIRTY-FOUR

The next day Cedric came in again before opening, rapping his knuckles on the door so that Ember would come up and unlock it.

"Coming to take me away?" she asked grimly.

"Oh please," he said. "I wouldn't dream of tackling you without backup." He had that dry, sarcastic tone, the same one Ember knew people often mistook for seriousness. Although the joke made her uneasy, she was a little relieved by the fact that he had made a joke at all.

Maybe that meant that he wasn't halfway to imagining her as a mass murderer.

Or maybe it just meant he was really good at pretending to trust people. Ember imagined the fake-joking act got people to let down their defenses, let their secrets out. Coming from someone as intimidating as Cedric, it probably worked like a charm.

Except that I don't have any secrets, Ember's racing mind objected. *But how am I supposed to convince him of that when I've got so much evidence stacked against me?*

Still, Ember reasoned, Cedric must have come to the bar for some purpose. She waited him out, watching him carefully as he paced, seemingly without aim, amongst the tables and chairs, craning his neck to look around the space.

"Just heard from the ME," Cedric said eventually. "That's the medical examiner, by the way."

"I know what it is," Ember said. "What did they say?"

"They determined that Laura, who was driving, was dead before the car hit that tree." He had turned to watch Ember carefully, as though trying to gage her reaction to this information. She felt suddenly very self-conscious about the expression her face was making.

"Dead *before* the crash?" Ember asked. "I mean, I guess that explains the crash."

"I guess so."

"And the others?"

Cedric hesitated, still watching Ember, calculating. She wondered what his extra shifter's senses were telling him about her right now. If he could somehow smell or hear the fact that she was telling the truth. That she sincerely didn't know what had happened to them.

"They died after the crash," he said eventually. "But not because of it."

"This is starting to sound like a riddle."

"The accident wasn't serious enough to have caused any of the deaths. Injuries, maybe. I bet they would have racked up a pretty serious chiropractor's bill, sure. But if those women had been otherwise healthy and well, there's no way that the impact would have left them all dead."

"So what did?"

"The ME doesn't know just yet," Cedric admitted. "She performed the autopsy on all three of them. She's sending some elements off for testing--I'm sure you'll be shocked to know that we don't have all the fanciest equipment here in town, some of the more obscure procedures need to be outsourced, and they end up in a long queue and we never get priority. But as of now, there's no official account as to what killed any of them."

Ember huffed a sigh. She wanted to be pleasant, to make Cedric's job easier on him by cooperating. But she also didn't like to hear that it might be a while before they had any answers.

"I'm sure you're not happy to hear that," he said, a little too carefully.

It also meant: *Are you happy to hear that?*

If she was the killer, she'd certainly be pleased to know that there would be such a long delay. Was he really that suspicious of her, that he didn't believe she wanted the truth to be discovered?

"Listen," she said, doing her best to keep her voice level and pleasant, "I know you've got a tough job to do here. This is a really upsetting event and there's a lot to be figured out. But I am *right* in the crosshairs. It's only a matter of time before people stop coming around here."

"I heard you did a good business last night."

She shrugged. She didn't need to make the point that it wouldn't last if people really started to think her pub was deadly, or cursed, or run by a homicidal maniac.

"That's actually what I came here for," he admitted after a pause. "I wanted to ask if you'd consider closing your pub until we can figure out what happened. It would be good for you, too, to take some time off, lie low. You look a little strained."

Ember frowned. "As much as I'd love to kick my feet up with a book and go to the spa for the foreseeable future, I really can't afford to do that. The Broken Broom is my livelihood."

He shrugged. "You might find it a little less profitable than it's worth to keep running, is all I'm saying."

"And all I'm saying is that you can't force me to close, can you? You don't have any real proof that those people died because of me. Everything is circumstantial. You're not ordering me to do anything, right?"

He shook his head. "Just a friendly suggestion."

"All right," she said. "Suggestion noted. But I'm going to stay open."

He huffed out a frustrated breath like they'd just argued, even though she'd worked so hard to keep the tone civil. Was he really so concerned for her?

Or concerned *about* her?

As he turned to leave, he shot back over his shoulder, "You know, if your customers keep dying after they visit your pub, you're going to lose everything anyway. Closing up could be a way of protecting yourself, too."

Before she really had the time to take that in, he was gone, the door swinging shut behind him.

ONCE SHE WAS ALONE with her thoughts and her opening checklist, Ember put her body to the task of wiping down menus and wrapping silverware sets and her mind to the task of thinking through what might have happened to those women--and Jake, too, if he was involved in this somehow.

The only thing that united all four of them was, potentially, the wine.

And she knew that Lyndsy hated all three of the women. She hardly made a secret of it.

But Lyndsy had poured the wine right in front of Ember. She wouldn't have had time to do anything to tamper with it.

Would she?

TO KEEP READING, click here!

Life's A Witch

Bottom Witch

Boss Witch

Payback's A Witch